He found her wanting....

"It's a very—nauseating experience, learning that your life has been put under someone else's microscope—and found wanting!"

"There was a good reason for that!"

"I'm sure there was," Sophie scorned. "I wonder just how close a scrutiny your own life would bear without—"

"We aren't discussing me," he told her stiffly.

"I know that I judge a person on what I find them to be, not on what some cold-blooded report tells me about them," she challenged.

"Cold-blooded," he repeated in a silkily soft voice. "Is that what you consider me?"

"Oh!" she gasped as she was suddenly pulled up against the hard length of his body, the warmth of his hands against the base of her spine. At that moment he felt anything but cold!

CAROLE MORTIMER is the youngest of three children and grew up in a small Bedfordshire village with her parents and two brothers. She still loves nothing more than going "home" to visit her family. In her mid-thirties, she now has a husband, three very active sons, four cats and a dog, which doesn't leave her a lot of time for hobbies! Her strong, traditional stories, with their distinctly modern appeal, fascinating characters and involving plots, have earned her an enthusiastic audience worldwide.

Books by Carole Mortimer

HARLEQUIN PRESENTS PLUS
1559—THE JILTED BRIDEGROOM
1583—PRIVATE LIVES
1607—MOTHER OF THE BRIDE
1631—ELUSIVE OBSESSION

HARLEQUIN PRESENTS
1227—THE LOVING GIFT
1258—ELUSIVE AS THE UNICORN
1325—A CHRISTMAS AFFAIR
1451—MEMORIES OF THE PAST
1468—ROMANCE OF A LIFETIME
1543—SAVING GRACE

CAROLE MORTIMER

Gracious Lady

Harlequin Books

TORONTO • NEW YORK • LONDON
AMSTERDAM • PARIS • SYDNEY • HAMBURG
STOCKHOLM • ATHENS • TOKYO • MILAN
MADRID • WARSAW • BUDAPEST • AUCKLAND

For Frank,
as always, with love

ISBN 0-373-11657-8

GRACIOUS LADY

Copyright © 1993 by Carole Mortimer.

CHAPTER ONE

'How dare you?' Sophie had cried with righteous indignation. 'Stop this car immediately and let me out!'

And what had the heartless swine done?

Stopped the car immediately and almost *pushed* her out on to the grass verge beside the road!

Which was precisely why, at this moment, she was walking along that very same road at almost one o'clock in the morning, cursing all men, and Brian Burnett in particular. What a louse, what an absolute pig, leaving her out here in the middle of nowhere—even if that was exactly what she had ordered him to do. Men never—at least, not the ones she had experience of!—did what you asked them to do. Except Brian Burnett, obviously! Although she was aware he had acted out of pique and not through any desire to be obliging; she hadn't been willing to give him what he wanted, and so he had been perfectly happy to stop his car and let her get out, driving off at great speed and leaving her there.

And he hadn't come back, damn him. Most men would have realised, eventually, just what a swine they had been just to dump her here in the middle of nowhere, but she had been walking for almost fifteen minutes now, and there was no sign of car headlights returning towards her.

Swine. Pig. Swine. Pig. She muttered the two names alternately with each step she took.

She just hoped her aunt Millie had left the back door open for her, or she was really going to be popular, arriving at one-thirty in the morning, which she had calculated it was going to be by the time she got back, and having to drag her aunt out of bed to let her in!

Maybe she shouldn't have gone out at all tonight, but her friend Ally had called, and it had been so long since she had seen her, and—God, how her feet ached in these high-heeled shoes she was unaccustomed to wearing. She couldn't remember the last time she had worn them, or a skirt either for that matter—denims and T-shirts were her usual mode of dress. But Ally had said they would be going out for a drink in a local pub, and so she had made the effort and put on a green blouse, which she had tucked into the narrow waistband of her brown skirt.

There was a car coming! She could see the headlights clearly as it approached—from a direction opposite to the one it would have been if it were Brian returning for her after all. And she was all alone here, she reminded herself hurriedly, her first feelings of relief fading fast; what if the driver of this car were even worse than Brian had been? Of course, the driver of this car could always be a woman—— No, not the way her luck was running tonight, it couldn't!

Too late; while she had been dithering about wondering what to do for the best, the car had already reached her, whooshing to a halt beside her as the driver must have seen her reflected in his headlights. Oh, God, let the driver be friendly!

'Are you asking to be raped?''

Not *that* friendly, Sophie gulped. No woman asked to be raped. But this man, his face thrown into sharp, shadowed profile by the eerie green light given off by the dashboard of his car, his voice a harshly cold rasp of accusation, obviously believed that, by wandering about country roads in the middle of the night, that was exactly what she was asking for!

'Or worse!' he continued relentlessly, his eyes glittering in the darkness.

He was trying to frighten her—wasn't he...? Well, he needn't bother, because she was already frightened!

'Get in the car,' he ordered abruptly, his tone brooking no argument.

Get in the——! She might be slightly stupid, but she wasn't completely witless. Once she got inside his car she would be completely at his mercy. 'I think I should warn you——' she raised her small pointed chin defensively, drawing herself up to her full height of five feet two inches '—that I've studied karate.' Hadn't everyone seen at least one of the cult films on the subject? She only hoped she wouldn't actually be put to the test of demonstrating just how much she had 'studied' it, because it certainly didn't amount to much.

'That's nice for you—now get in the car!' The instruction was repeated with harsh impatience, completely nullifying his initially mild tone.

Sophie swallowed hard, frantically trying to estimate how far she would get if she ran in the high heels that were already crippling her feet—she was sure she had blisters on her toes—before he could put the car back into gear and catch up with her. The alternative, of attempting to cross fields on a less-than-moonlit night, she had dismissed almost as soon as it entered her head. It would just be pure madness on her part even to try to get away from this man that way. But she didn't think she was going to get very far by running either; the car engine sounded powerful even though it was only ticking over at the moment, and she would probably just antagonise this man even further by putting him to the trouble of having to come after her. Oh, God, she didn't know what to do, and she could feel his impatience with her increasing by the second.

'You either get in the car and let me drive you into the village, or I call the police and put them to the trouble of coming out to pick you up,' he warned in a danger-ously soft voice.

'Oh, yes!' Sophie pounced eagerly on the latter suggestion. Not that she actually intended remaining here to get picked up by the police; Aunt Millie would have a fit if she was driven back in a police car! But if she could just get this man to leave, she could make sure she was well away from here by the time the police came along. 'That sounds like a great idea,' she encouraged enthusiastically. 'There's a telephone in the village——'

'I have a car phone,' he cut in derisively.

A car phone! Why hadn't she thought of that? Damn modern technology! A few years ago it hadn't been possible to telephone anyone from the confines of your car; now it seemed almost everyone had the convenience of a car phone. It was just her luck that this man should have one—— Perhaps that was *just* what it was... She could always call his bluff about using the phone, and that way she would know too whether he genuinely wanted to give her a lift to the village or if he was just using the idea of it as a way of getting her inside the car.

'Then perhaps I could use it to call my aunt?' she suggested lightly, not wanting to antagonise him—es-pecially as her claim to being a karate expert had been pure invention!

She cursed the fact that the darkness prevented her being able to see him properly, but, even so, she could see he was a big man by the amount of space he took up inside the car, and his voice sounded strong and authoritative, as if he was used to issuing orders—and having them obeyed! She had probably already annoyed him intensely by not doing as she was told.

'I'm a little later than I told my aunt I would be,' Sophie explained ruefully. 'And she'll be worried about me.' The truth of the matter was her aunt wouldn't be worrying about her at all, because she would assume Sophie had come in and gone to bed hours ago. And she would be deeply upset to realise that wasn't the case at all. But Aunt Millie's displeasure seemed the lesser of two evils at the moment!

'I would be worried about you too if you were my niece,' the man told her disparagingly. 'Here.' The car phone was thrust up in front of her nose. 'Just dial the number and wait for the connection,' he instructed wearily as she hesitated.

'Wait' seemed to be the operative word, her assumption that her aunt had already gone to bed seeming to be the correct one as the telephone rang and rang unanswered at the other end of the line. 'She's probably fallen asleep waiting up for me,' Sophie told the man hastily as she sensed his growing impatience.

'I wouldn't be in the least surprised,' he murmured critically, condemnation in his voice.

Sophie didn't know what gave him the right to be so critical about her; if he weren't up and still out at this time of night then the two of them wouldn't be having this conversation at all. And there were a limited number of reasons why one might be out this late in this area . . . Which was obviously why he seemed only too happy to make assumptions concerning her own presence here.

'I'm sure she'll hear the telephone ringing in a minute—Oh, Aunt Millie!' she cried out thankfully as the receiver was at last picked up the other end and she heard the reassuringly familiar sound of her aunt's voice on the other end of the line. Although her aunt's reaction when she realised it was Sophie making the call wasn't quite so reassuring—as she had feared it might not be!

'What on earth——? Do you realise what time it is?' her aunt demanded indignantly as she obviously came fully awake. 'Where are you? What are you still doing out at this time of night; I thought you had gone to bed ages ago. Sophie, this is really too much——'

'I realise how worried you are, Aunt Millie,' Sophie cut in, her voice lightly cajoling, purely for the benefit of the man sitting inside the car so obviously listening. What she actually said was for his benefit too; at the moment her aunt was obviously more angry than worried about her. Not that she could exactly blame her; her aunt, whenever it was possible to do so, liked to retire early for the night, and had probably been asleep for hours before the telephone rang so intrusively. 'I just wanted to let you know I'll be home soon, and that——'

'You got me out of bed at this hour just to tell me you'll be home soon?' Aunt Millie said incredulously. 'Sophie——'

'Yes, that's right,' she continued the act. 'Um—Ally was delayed in town, and so I'm getting a lift back with—with another friend.' This conversation was very awkward, to say the least. She wanted to reassure her aunt without actually alarming her, while at the same time letting this man know that someone knew where she was and was expecting her home within the next half-hour, which was the most it should take to drive back from town.

'What friend?' her aunt said sharply. 'Sophie, you've only been here a day,' she continued exasperatedly. 'And already you're causing chaos!'

'What friend . . . ?' Sophie repeated slowly, thinking fast, knowing she was just making the situation worse with her half-truths and evasions. 'His name is——'

'Maximilian Grant,' the man supplied quietly from inside the car.

'Ma—Brian Burnett!' Sophie frantically replaced, staring inside the car with horrified fascination. Oh, my

God, Maximilian Grant. Of all the people who could possibly have stopped, it had to be *him*! Thank God she hadn't just blurted his name out to her aunt; that would really have put the cat among the pigeons. 'Er—Brian Burnett,' she repeated in a calmer voice, turning away from the car now. 'You remember him,' she spoke quickly, desperately trying to think of a way out of this situation—there wasn't one! A hard knot of misery formed in the bottom of her stomach; she could never remember outstaying her welcome in a matter of hours before. 'Ally's brother,' she added vaguely.

Maximilian Grant! She still couldn't believe her luck. Anyone else and it wouldn't have mattered; but him? Oh, lord!

'Of course I remember him,' her aunt answered impatiently. 'He's been——'

'Look I'll have to go, Aunt Millie,' Sophie cut her off quickly. 'I'll be back soon, and we can talk then.'

'I am going to bed, Sophie,' her aunt told her in no uncertain terms. 'We will talk in the morning.'

And Sophie knew her aunt well enough by now to know that when she said *they* would talk in the morning, what she actually meant was that *she* would talk and Sophie would listen. And learn. Or else. It was ridiculous that at twenty-two she should still be in awe of her aunt Millie and the undoubtably sharp edge of her tongue, but it was a lesson she had learnt the hard way during long summer holidays with her aunt's family when she was a child. If anything, her aunt had become sharper over the years, not mellowed! And she didn't have her cousin Arlette to act as a buffer between her aunt's impatience with her impetuosity this time either, Arlette being away in Germany at the moment.

'Er—I don't have a key to get in,' Sophie muttered reluctantly into the mouthpiece of the telephone, her mind racing all the time as she wondered exactly what she was going to do about the man sitting inside the car, impatience emanating from him now at the delay.

But her panic concerning him was of a different kind now, for she no longer feared his motives in stopping; this man certainly wasn't about to attempt to rape or murder her. However, he did have a power over her life that——

'Well, really!' her aunt said incredulously. 'You really are the limit, Sophie. I would have thought you would have matured the last few years, given all that's happened to you, but I can see from your behaviour tonight that you're just as irresponsible as you ever were! I should never——'

'You'll wait up for me,' Sophie feigned gratitude for the non-existent offer, at the same time wondering why it was that these things did happen to her.

She had gone out tonight to meet Ally in all innocence, had looked forward to seeing her old childhood friend, and because of that her plans for the next week could now all be lost. And she had needed that week. Hell! It was all Brian Burnett's fault. This would teach her to wonder if she still had the crush on him that she had at thirteen. Three years older than Ally, Arlette, and herself, he had seemed like a god all those years ago. He was a god that had matured to have feet of clay. He—— She frowned as she saw another car coming, in the opposite direction this time, headlights blazing in the darkness.

'I'll see you soon, Aunt Millie,' she added quickly, ending the call before her aunt could protest at the suggestion.

She had no doubt her aunt was going to be furious when she did get back, but one awkward situation at a time; she had Maximilian Grant to deal with first! How to get herself out of this situation, she just didn't know. Once he realised who she was...

'Now get in the car,' he instructed tersely as she handed him the portable phone, revving the engine of the car in preparation of leaving.

She hadn't been able to see who he was in the darkness; she would have recognised him instantly if it had been daylight—his harsh good looks, blond hair shot through with silver, ice-cold blue eyes, photographed often in the newspapers. But now that she knew he was Maximilian Grant she felt even less inclined to get in the car with him! If she hadn't been able to see him well enough to recognise him, maybe if she could evade spending any more time in his company he wouldn't recognise her when he saw her again either. When. Because they *would* meet again. And in very different circumstances. If only——

The car that had fast been approaching from the opposite direction suddenly dazzled her with its headlights. Oh, God, so much for her being in the darkness and so unrecognisable; her hair now, she knew, would appear like a red flame in the bright lights. Completely distinctive. Unforgettable. The other car was stopping too now; not one 'gallant knight' wanting to help a 'lady in distress', but two! But she couldn't see this second driver any better than she had Maximilian Grant, could just make out a bulky outline seated behind the wheel of the car.

'Sophie, I'm sorry.' But she recognised the male voice only too well this time. Brian! He had come back for her after all. 'I behaved like a fool before.' He had switched off the engine of his car, got out of the car, and was crossing the road towards her now. 'I got all the way home before I realised how stupidly I had——'

'It doesn't matter,' she cut in hastily, moving forward to grasp hold of his arm and stop him before he could reach the side of Maximilian Grant's car. 'What matters is that you're here now. Get back in your car and I'll join you in a minute. I just have to thank this kind gentleman for stopping, and then I'll be right with you.' She had turned Brian in the direction of his car as she spoke, pushing him towards it now.

And he didn't want to be pushed! 'But——'

'Wait in the car, Brian,' she instructed tautly, anxious the two men shouldn't meet. Then it would be all over for her.

'But—but——' Again he did a good impression of a stalled engine.

'*I said wait in the car, Brian.*' Her near-desperation was barely controlled this time.

'All right, all right!' He shrugged off her hands, as if he didn't know what all the fuss was about anyway. 'God, I only came back to apologise,' he could be heard muttering as he returned to his car. 'Women!' he added disgustedly as he climbed in behind the wheel, slamming the door behind him.

He had better not drive off again now! Because if he did, the next time she saw him she would strangle him, Ally's brother or not!

'Your lover appears to be still somewhat irate,' Maximilian Grant drawled mockingly from the interior of his car. 'Are you sure you want to go with him?'

The arrogant——! 'Brian isn't my lover,' she told him indignantly—and then wondered why she was bothering. She was just prolonging the conversation, and increasing the possibility of recognition when they met again; she should just have thanked him politely for stopping, and made a dignified exit.

He was looking up at her in the darkness now; she could almost feel that penetrating gaze on her. No wonder he was so successful in business, if the power in his eyes could be felt under these circumstances; it must be quite wilting for business associates to feel the full force of those icy blue eyes upon them.

'No?' he drawled sceptically in reply to her claim. 'I gathered from the conversation between the two of you just now that your walking alone along this road at this time of the night is the result of a lovers' tiff,' he added harshly, having continued determinedly on when Sophie opened her mouth to protest once again at this description of Brian's role in her life; she hadn't even seen Brian for years until tonight—that had been partly why his behaviour earlier had so outraged her! 'I would give serious thought,' Maximilian Grant told her grimly, 'as to whether or not you want to continue a relationship with a man who threw you out of his car in the middle of nowhere at half-past twelve at night!'

Sophie gasped indignantly. 'He didn't throw me out, I made him stop the car and let me out! And if I hadn't been defending——' She broke off with a self-consciously indrawn breath as she realised what she had been about to say.

'Nevertheless, one presumes he gave you reason for such an action, and the result was totally irresponsible—on the part of both of you, it would seem,' Maximilian Grant rasped critically.

She winced at his use of the word 'irresponsible'. The last thing she wanted this man to think her was irresponsible.

'You could have lost a lot more than your "honour" wandering around deserted roads this time of night,' he warned impatiently, showing her immediately that he had drawn his own conclusions about what she had been about to claim she was defending earlier. And as it happened he was completely wrong; she would have had no trouble 'defending her honour' with Brian, and certainly wouldn't have ended up walking back because of it! 'I would suggest that in future, you choose your friends a little more carefully,' he added harshly.

It sounded more like an order than a suggestion, actually, but as it appeared to be his parting comment, he putting the car into gear now and driving off with smooth efficiency, Sophie didn't particularly care how it sounded. She was just glad he had finally left. She could breathe again now, felt as if she had been hyperventilating since the moment the man had revealed his identity as Maximilian Grant. 'Of all the cars in all the world'; not quite the original quote, but it was apt. So very apt!

'Sophie, could we get moving now?' Brian had wound his car window down to prompt impatiently. 'I know it's the weekend tomorrow, but I still have to go to work, and it's late——'

'Well, lucky old you!' she ground out furiously as she marched across the road to wrench open the passenger door—such a gentleman to get out and open the door for her, she didn't think!—and got in beside him. 'Thanks to you I—oh, never mind.' She glared across the width of the car at him. 'Just drive, will you?' She hunched down in her seat. 'I'm no more anxious to spend any more time in your company than you are in mine!' She scowled unseeingly ahead of her.

'I didn't say—— Oh, all right,' Brian sighed wearily as the fierceness of her glowering glare was turned on him. 'But it seems to me you're making an awful fuss about this whole business,' he muttered to himself as he accelerated the car forward. 'I made a mistake. I've apologised. I don't know why we can't just forget the whole incident,' he added in a disgruntled voice.

That was the whole point; he had no idea that she would probably not be allowed to forget it! Aunt Millie, waiting up for her at home, wasn't likely to let her forget it in a hurry. And to her mind, much more significantly, there was Maximilian Grant...

'Ally is going to kill me,' Brian sighed wearily as Sophie didn't confirm or deny his previous suggestion.

Remembering the fiery temper of her friend from childhood, Sophie wouldn't be in the least surprised! 'It's no more than you deserve,' she told Brian now, although her tension had already started to diminish. 'I should just let Ally have you,' she added teasingly. 'But I won't!' She gave a rueful smile now at the thought of it. 'It would be a little like throwing you to the lions!' She shook her head. 'I can't actually see any reason why Ally has to know about this at all.' The fewer people who knew anything about tonight, the better; too many people knew about it already as far as she was concerned.

'Thanks!' Brian said with obvious relief for the reprieve—his gratitude having the effect of making Sophie feel somewhat guilty now, when she was just as anxious that the incident should be kept between the two of them. 'My sister can be a real nag when she wants to be.' He frowned at the thought.

Talking of nags...she had better start thinking of what she was going to say to Aunt Millie when she got back!

Sophie fell silent again just at the thought of it, her return of good humour fading too. By the time Aunt Millie had finished with her, she doubted she would have much to smile about!

And so it was no surprise at all, as they approached the house, to see it ablaze with lights. 'Just drop me off here,' Sophie told Brian as they turned in the driveway, the house still some distance away. 'Ally has nothing on my aunt Millie when it comes to the "outraged dragon",' she explained with a grimace at his questioning look. 'And as you can see by the lights, she's still up!'

Sophie could envisage her aunt right now, seated at the wooden table in the centre of the kitchen, the belt

to her pink towelling bathrobe neatly tied at her ample
waist, her rosy face bare of make-up, even the powder
and lipstick she usually wore during the day, and there
would possibly be rollers in her hair, depending on
whether or not tonight was a hair-wash night; Sophie
wasn't sure about the latter, had left too early in the
evening to know one way or the other. But she did know
her aunt wouldn't be reading or writing, or doing anything else for that matter, as she waited. She would just
be waiting.

Brian didn't need any further discouragement,
stopping the car while they were still well away from the
house, turning in his seat to look at her. 'If you'd like
me to come in with you, I will,' he offered bravely.

Sophie laughed softly. 'Now I know why I had a crush
on you when I was younger! It's a nice offer, Brian, and
I do appreciate it.' She squeezed his arm gratefully. 'But
I believe Aunt Millie is best faced alone.' Mainly because, in this instance, Brian was more likely to drop
her further into trouble than she already was if he should
say the wrong thing at the wrong time!

As it was, Sophie was still trying to work out what
she could say to her aunt—if she had a chance to say
anything!

'If you're sure that's what you'd prefer...' Brian accepted with some relief. 'I'll call you in a few days, shall
I, and—no?' He winced as he saw she was already
shaking her head at the suggestion.

'We're friends again, Brian; let's just leave it at that,'
Sophie dismissed evenly. 'And don't try this on anyone
else, hmm?' she advised as she pushed the car door open
in preparation of getting out onto the gravelled driveway.
'You aren't very good at it!'

'Thanks!' he returned drily. 'A man's ego certainly
couldn't become inflated with you around, could it!'

She chuckled softly before shutting the door and
setting off down the driveway, grateful to Brian as she
did so as he deliberately kept the car headlights brightly
shining in that direction until she reached the door; it
was a black, moonless night, and shadowy bushes edged
the driveway in eerie silence.

She turned and waved once she reached the door,
vaguely registering that Brian was turning the car around
and leaving now even as she saw, from the light streaming
from the kitchen window, that sleek car of bottle-green
parked outside. Sophie's nervousness returned anew at
the sight of that car, and she entered the house on leaden
feet.

As soon as she entered the kitchen she could see she
was wrong on all four counts concerning her aunt; she
wasn't seated at the table but stood beside it putting a
cup and saucer on a tray, she wasn't dressed for bed but
wore one of her usual blue dresses with the pristine white
collar, and her powder and lipstick looked newly applied, and, although Sophie could see her aunt *had*
washed her hair, it certainly wasn't in rollers but neatly
brushed into style.

Oh, well, here goes, Sophie groaned inwardly. 'Aunt
Millie?'

Her aunt was so startled, obviously not having heard
Sophie's entrance, that she almost dropped the sugar
bowl she had been about to put on the tray with the cup
and saucer. She glared across at Sophie impatiently at
the same time she slammed the sugar bowl down. 'I
didn't hear you get back,' she accused unnecessarily, her
attention almost immediately returning to the tray,
adding a coffee-pot and a jug of cream before nodding
her satisfaction that everything seemed to be in place.

'Just now,' Sophie nodded warily. 'Brian brought me
back.' And this time she wasn't lying! 'Aunt Millie, I
want to explain about——'

'Not now, Sophie,' her aunt dismissed irritably, picking up the tray. 'Can't you see I'm busy?'

Of course she could see her aunt was busy, but it was imperative she explain to her about——

Her aunt frowned. 'If you want to do something useful, Sophie, then open the door for me so that I can——'

'Mrs Craine, I've decided I will have that sandwich you offered, after all.' The door to the main part of the house had been thrust open from the other side before Sophie could reach it, a man now standing in the doorway.

A man with harshly hewn good looks, blond hair shot through with silver, and ice-cold blue eyes . . .

CHAPTER TWO

MAXIMILIAN GRANT.

The owner of this house and the extensive grounds that surrounded it. Her aunt's employer. And he had arrived unexpectedly in the middle of the night.

Sophie had recognised his voice immediately he spoke as he opened the door, of course, had frozen in her position slightly behind that door—which was probably the reason he didn't seem to have seen her yet!

Would he recognise her when he did see her?

Recognise her as what, she wondered with a grimace? The young woman he had come across alone in the dark at the side of the road, apparently 'asking to be raped or worse'?

What else was it he had called her? 'irresponsible', and—oh, God, he'd said she should choose her friends more wisely in future. And she was supposed to be here as the prospective companion, for the following week, to his young daughter! After the unforgettable list of offences he had already found her guilty of, she didn't think that was very likely to happen now.

She gave a weary sigh at the thought of having to pack up her things and leave again so soon after she had got here; she had only arrived that very afternoon. But she now gave up all hope that Maximilian Grant wouldn't realise she had been that woman walking along the road in the dark; if she had recognised his voice instantly, then it was logical to assume he would recognise hers too, especially as the incident was still so new. And memorable. At least, she presumed he didn't stop along dark country roads to offer lifts to 'damsels in distress' every night of the week! Or even if he did—although he certainly hadn't given the impression of being a knight in shining armour!—they wouldn't all have turned out to be the woman seeking the position as companion to his daughter.

Sophie couldn't help the grin that spread across her face as a perfectly ludicrous idea occurred to her. It must be the near-hysteria she felt at this whole situation that was causing it, but she had suddenly had an illusion of Mr Rochester with a car phone! OK, so she was taking poetic licence with the story, but there was no denying that they *had* met in the dark of night, nor that Maximilian Grant had been travelling, albeit in a car rather than on horseback, to his country home, nor that she was here as the companion he hadn't yet met to his young charge, this time a daughter rather than a ward.

OK, she was taking *more* than poetic licence with this last bit; Maximilian Grant's daughter Jennifer wasn't home from school for the week's half-term holiday until tomorrow, and Sophie had yet to be officially given the job of keeping her occupied for the week. Another twist, a rather significant one in this case, was that Sophie was the one who had actually realised Maximilian Grant's identity, rather than the other way around, as it had been with Rochester and Jane. Perhaps not Mr Rochester with a car phone after all...

She had been trying to cheer herself up with this non-sense, and now she realised she just felt more deflated than ever. Not depressed. She had made a vow to herself long ago that she wouldn't allow that emotion to colour her life. As she didn't boredom either. There was always something to see, too much to do, to give in to that malaise. But, even so, she realised that this time she was coming very close to it!

'Roast chicken?'

It took Sophie several seconds to realise her aunt was answering her employer's request for a sandwich. Her aunt had been expecting Maximilian Grant in the morning, had been cooking his favourite foods all day in preparation for the weekend, her employer having spent the weekdays in his London apartment, as he usually did. Much to Aunt Millie's chagrin; there was nothing she liked better than having someone to look after and feed. She had complained to Sophie only that afternoon, as she bustled about cooking pies and cakes, that she was sure Maximilian Grant didn't look after himself properly in London anyway, that she didn't understand why he didn't spend more time down here. It wasn't the same for her now as it had been with the last owners of Henley Hall, the Grays and their three children permanently in residence. But the Grays had sold up to Maximilian Grant over a year ago, and, although Aunt Millie had been asked to stay on as cook-housekeeper, she didn't enjoy it now as much as she had when the Grays and their three young children had lived here. Maybe now that Maximilian Grant and his daughter were both back...

'That will be fine,' he accepted tersely now. 'I'll take the coffee tray back with——' He broke off suddenly, turning sharply, pinning Sophie with those ice-blue eyes, his mouth thinning. 'I didn't realise you had company.' He turned back to her aunt almost accusingly.

Sophie's tentative grin, on at last being spotted, turned into a sickly grimace at the open hostility in his voice now. Gone was the abruptly polite employer who had been talking to her aunt, and in his place was—Sophie wasn't sure...

He must have known the person he was thinking of employing as Jennifer's companion was coming here, because he had asked that she be here for an interview on Saturday morning before his daughter came home from boarding-school at lunchtime, and he also knew she was his housekeeper's niece, so that couldn't be the problem either. And yet he was reacting to her presence here now as if she were some sort of intruder. It didn't make sense. She hadn't even spoken yet, so it couldn't be that!

'I'm Sophie Gordon,' she decided to take the initiative when her aunt seemed as surprised by his attitude towards her as she was, stepping forward to hold her hand out in polite greeting. 'Aunt Mil—er—Mrs Craine's niece,' she hastily amended at her aunt's frown, the beginnings of a blush darkening her cheeks as she saw Maximilian Grant's eyes narrow even more, in puzzlement this time.

Her voice! He *did* recognise her voice, was looking her up and down critically now.

And Sophie knew exactly what he would see: a shock of short red curls that refused to be tamed, huge hazel-coloured eyes that could be either green or brown, depending on her mood—right now they were definitely green!—a small snub nose, generously curving mouth, a determinedly pointed chin, her slight, almost boyish body clothed in the unaccustomed skirt and blouse, the satiny sheen to the latter being what had made it easy earlier for him to spot her in the headlights of his car. Well, at least she had done something sensible tonight, had worn something—even if it had been unintentionally at the time!—that could be clearly seen. Although she doubted 'sensible' was the word going through Maximilian Grant's mind at the moment concerning her; she was already well aware of what he thought of her! But Aunt Millie wasn't, and——

'Ah, yes,' Maximilian Grant answered her slowly, the hostility gone now—to be replaced with dry mockery. 'You're here about the job,' he nodded tauntingly.

And she could kiss goodbye to that job, Sophie read from the derisive glint in his eyes, her arm falling back to her side as he made no effort to shake her hand. Which meant that she could also say goodbye to the week's wages too. And she had needed that money. She doubted, in the circumstances, that he would feel like reimbursing her return train fare either, which made all of this a double blow. Well, she might just have to ask him for the latter; she couldn't afford, literally, to be proud.

'That's right,' she confirmed brightly. 'I came down by train this afternoon so that I wouldn't be late for our interview in the morning.'

Dark blond brows rose over mocking eyes. 'Very commendable, I'm sure,' he drawled softly. 'Although it could be called taking punctuality to the extreme!'

She felt the heat in her cheeks at his undoubted sarcasm at her expense. 'I thought it would be nice to spend some time with my aunt before—if my time here were to be taken up with Jennifer for the next week,' she defended with a shrug—and then wished she hadn't bothered as the mockery deepened in his expression, wry amusement quirking a mouth that looked as if it could border on cruelty if crossed. Border? Go well over the edge!

'Really?' Maximilian Grant murmured now, his stance challenging, his legs slightly apart, wearing dark fitted trousers that looked as if they might be part of a well-cut business suit, his snowy-white shirt unbuttoned at the neck, although he had probably worn a tie with it earlier; he didn't look the type to dress casually very often, and today had been a working day. The tie would have been silk too, Sophie guessed ruefully; Maximilian Grant's business empire had made him a millionaire many times over. 'And did the two of you have a pleasant evening together talking over family and old times?' he enquired pleasantly now.

Too pleasantly! He knew, damn him—she was sure now that he did!—that she hadn't spent the evening with her aunt at all, believed she had spent them in the arms of her lover, Brian Burnett!

But, Sophie puzzled with a frown, as he did know that, and they both knew that he did, why didn't he just tell her aunt? Whatever his reason, she was sure it had nothing to do with helping her avoid the severe verbal reprimand she would get from her aunt if she were to be told Sophie had already made the acquaintance of her employer, and under circumstances Aunt Millie certainly wouldn't approve of!

"We spent the afternoon catching up on family news," her aunt was the one to answer him in perfect innocence of the taunt, obviously pleased at how well Sophie and her employer appeared to be getting on together. She had actually recommended Sophie for this job, and would feel it reflected badly on her if Sophie should now prove unsuitable.

Unsuitable, Sophie realised with an inward groan, had to be the very *least* of what Maximilian Grant thought of her. Although the most she could hope for was that he wouldn't be too frank with her aunt when he told her that!

'Sophie spent the evening with a friend she made down here during holidays with us as a child,' her aunt added affectionately.

'Indeed?' Eyes so pale a blue that they looked almost grey were narrowed on Sophie now even as he answered her aunt's statement. 'Perhaps you would bring the tray through to my study and we can talk now.' All humour had gone from his expression now, derisive as it had been, and he was grimly authoritative, the suggestion an order rather than a request. 'Another cup, if you please, Mrs Craine.'

One-thirty in the morning hardly seemed like the ideal time to be conducting an interview, Sophie thought even as she was vaguely aware of her aunt putting another cup on the tray. But despite the realisation that she now felt rather tired, from travelling down here today, an evening out that had hardly been uneventful, and the very lateness of the hour, Sophie knew she was in no position to argue, so she picked up the tray dutifully in preparation for following him.

He arched dark blond brows. 'Are you hungry? Or is that a silly question to ask a student? I believe you're reputed to be permanently in that state,' he said ruefully.

Sophie turned frowningly to her aunt Millie. She was taking a university course, yes, but she could hardly be classed as a student. Aunt Millie saw her puzzled look, giving a barely perceptible shake of her head in reply, and to Sophie's further discomfort she realised her aunt hadn't told Maximilian Grant the whole truth about her. Not that she could exactly blame her aunt, but it did put Sophie in a doubly awkward position where this man was concerned.

'I ate earlier, thank you,' she replied distractedly, frantically wondering exactly what her aunt Millie had told her employer about her.

'A chicken sandwich for one, then, Mrs Craine,' he instructed tersely before striding purposefully out of the room.

Sophie shot a helpless look across the room at her aunt before hurrying after him, the coffee-pot rattling precariously as she did so, forcing her to slow her pace or run the risk of throwing hot coffee all over this beautifully carpeted hallway.

During the days of Sophie's childhood holidays spent here, this house had been comfortably well-worn, the Grays having inherited the house rather than bought it, and with the expense of running such a large house, and

three boisterous children to provide for, the house, while
not exactly running into disrepair, had become worn and
faded, a financial burden the young couple had found
crippling, to the point where they had finally been able
to manage no longer.

The house looked far from worn and faded now, an
interior designer having been called in as soon as Henley
Hall became Maximilian Grant's. Workmen of all types
had quickly followed, and her aunt had complained that
for the next two months she had done nothing but
provide tea and coffee for the workmen and clear up the
mess they had made, all to the sound of their heaving
and banging and the smell of newly applied paint. The
result, Sophie had felt when she arrived here earlier
today, had to have been worth it.

The whole of the downstairs floor had been carpeted
in the same rich red and gold, the furniture all antique,
deep red velvet curtains at the huge windows, glittering
candelabra hanging from the high ceilings. Upstairs there
had been a bit more personality added to the choice,
Jennifer's room a froth of cream lace and silk, the master
bedroom more austere in dark and light blue, all of the
guest bedrooms—and there were six of them—
decorated in two-tonal colours that perfectly
complemented each other. Sophie was temporarily al-
lotted a bedroom near her aunt downstairs, until it was
decided whether or not she would be staying, neither of
them liking to make the assumption that she would be.
But, her aunt had briskly informed her, if she was taken
on, she would be moved up to one of the guest bedrooms, suitably close to Jennifer.

Sophie didn't think there was much likelihood of that
happening now!

She hadn't seen in Maximilian Grant's study earlier
when her aunt had taken her round to show her the
changes that had been made since her last visit just before

the Grays left last year, but its austere brown and cream décor, and heavy oak furniture, came as no surprise to her; it was exactly what she would have expected Maximilian Grant to have surrounded himself with as he worked.

Although...remembering how he hadn't told her aunt of the way he had met her on the road earlier, perhaps he wasn't as predictable as she thought he was!

With the minimum of fuss he made a space now on the brown leather-topped desk for the coffee-tray, and Sophie put it down gratefully, having been terrified that she would further disgrace herself by dropping it everywhere.

She wondered, as she straightened, if she should just say her piece and leave gracefully. But while there was still a chance of her having the job, even the slimmest of one—— Yet was there, really, or was this man just trying to let her down gently? If he was, it would probably be the first time he had ever been this considerate!

Maximilian Grant's success in business was legendary. He seemed to have interests in almost everything, from film companies, recording studios, airlines and newspapers, to race horses, the latter seeming to win for him with monotonous regularity. If Sophie were a gambler, which she most certainly wasn't, his were the horses she would bet on. But she didn't and his horses just went on winning without her money on them.

His personal life seemed to be no less successful. He'd escorted dozens of beautiful women since the death of his wife three years ago. Although none of them seemed, as yet, to have found a lasting place in the spot most people seemed to call a heart. In fact, one rather disgruntled actress, much in demand for her talent and beauty, who had ceased to hold his attention after only a matter of weeks, had claimed he didn't have a heart

at all, only a stone where it should have been! The fact
that simultaneously she had failed to get the leading role
in the latest film he was involved in producing might
have had something to do with the vitriolic outburst,
but even so it was no secret that Maximilian Grant didn't
have any inclination towards finding a second wife for
himself. And, to Sophie's mind, a man didn't gain the
coldly calculating reputation this man had in his business
and personal life without there being some truth in it.

'Would you like to "be Mother"?'

After her so recent thoughts about the intimate side
of his life, this mockingly drawled request came as
something of a shock! But then Sophie saw that his attention was fixed pointedly on the tray of coffee, as he
sat behind his desk, and she realised he only wanted her
to pour the steaming brew!

'Of course,' she returned smoothly, although once
again her cheeks felt hot, and from the way his taunting
gaze followed her slightly flustered movements with the
coffee-pot she almost felt as if he could read her mind.
Well, if that was the case, she hoped he could read now
that she thought he wasn't being fair to mock her in this
way, not when he already knew he had her at such a
disadvantage.

'Cream and sugar?' she enquired coolly, on her dignity
now.

His mouth seemed to twitch at her attempt to put
things back on a formal footing between them, and he
shook his head in curt refusal of the offer. 'I'll take it
just as it comes from the pot this time of night. I need
the caffeine,' he added ruefully.

He didn't look as if he 'needed' anything; he was as
alert and steely-eyed as if he had recently awoken from
a long refreshing sleep. Whereas she felt exhausted, certainly far from her sparkling best. Which was a mistake
on her part; she had a feeling it never paid to be less

than at one's best when up against this man. And at the moment, because he deliberately made himself such an enigma, she did feel they were antagonists.

'Your young man did bring you all the way home this time, then?'

Sophie drew her breath in sharply at the sharp edge to the question, sure in that moment that he had deliberately attempted to put her at her ease before by seeming to fall in with her wish to be the polite strangers they would have been if it hadn't been for that incident beside the road earlier. Now he was letting her know, with one sharp parry, that he had no intention of forgetting the incident, no matter what impression he might have given to the contrary in front of her aunt.

Sophie handed him his cup of coffee with a hand that shook slightly. Maybe it was as well she wasn't going to work for him after all. She liked to relax, enjoy herself where she worked, and this man's presence here would make that impossible for her.

'As you can see,' she nodded abruptly. 'I—thank you for not telling my aunt about that earlier,' she added stiffly, having dropped down into the chair opposite his across the desk.

He made no attempt to drink the coffee she had given him, putting the cup down on the desktop, his eyes narrowed to steely slits now as his gaze levelled on Sophie. 'I didn't do that to save you any embarrassment,' he told her harshly, 'but because I believed it might have upset your aunt to know about the ridiculous situation you had got yourself into. She seems very fond of you...'

Although he couldn't for the life of him understand why, when she was so obviously unworthy of the affection, his tone seemed to imply!

But she had been proved correct in her earlier belief that he hadn't been interested in protecting her by not telling her aunt they had already met, and under what circumstances.

'Look on the bright side,' Sophie returned. 'If I hadn't kept Aunt Millie up waiting to let me in because I didn't have a key, she wouldn't have been up and about to make your coffee and sandwich!'

His mouth thinned, his eyes ice-cold. 'I'm more than capable of getting my own coffee and sandwich,' he rasped harshly.

Sophie would hazard a guess at his being more than capable of doing most things for himself! She really shouldn't have let herself be goaded into giving that insolent reply. And she wouldn't have done if he weren't so—so damned superior, looking down that arrogant nose of his at her as if she were some unusual type of specimen that he wanted to push and poke around until he discovered what made her function the way that she did—and then dispose of her! Or maybe she was just being over-sensitive; after all, he did have a certain right to be judgemental about her behaviour...

'Or you could have made it for me,' he continued challengingly before she could make a reply. 'When you finally got in!'

She winced at the disapproving anger in his voice. He sounded like a stern father reprimanding a wayward child, although anyone less like her own wonderful, indulgent father she couldn't imagine—and she doubted Maximilian Grant would welcome the idea of her as his child any more favourably! Maybe prospective employer reprimanding a less than suitable candidate for employment was more like it, after all. And the longer they talked, the more she realised how true that probably was; she didn't 'suit' Maximilian Grant at all!

She moistened her lips nervously. 'You——'

'Sorry I took so long with your sandwich, Mr Grant.' Her aunt chose that moment to bustle into the room after the briefest of knocks to alert them to her presence, smiling at the two of them brightly as she came in, seeming unaware of the tension that fairly crackled in the room between her employer and her niece. At least, to Sophie it did! 'I made you some fresh mayonnaise to go with it,' Aunt Millie beamed with satisfaction.

'You shouldn't have gone to all that trouble, Mrs Craine.' Maximilian Grant relaxed enough to smile up at Sophie's aunt, although Sophie could see the angry glitter directed at her still in his ice-blue eyes. She had seen a photograph of an iceberg once that had the palest of blue coloration to it; this man's eyes reminded her of that iceberg. 'You really must go to bed now, Mrs Craine.' His smile took some of the order out of the sharpness of his words as he spoke to her aunt again, but it was no less an instruction he expected her to obey, for all that.

Even so, Sophie knew it was an order her aunt would have to disobey; there was no way Aunt Millie would just meekly go off to bed now, without learning exactly how Sophie had got on in her interview with Maximilian Grant. That was something she wasn't alone in!

'Sophie and I can clear away here when we're finished,' Maximilian Grant added—as if he was well aware of his housekeeper's reluctance.

'Very well,' Aunt Millie replied stiffly, making her exit, dignified displeasure down each rigid inch of her spine.

Sophie winced, knowing that look only too well. Not that it appeared to be bothering Maximilian Grant as he looked across the desk at Sophie with raised brows. And why should it bother him? The most Aunt Millie could do to him was serve him up an inedible meal, and as her aunt was very proud of her cooking, that wasn't very likely! Sophie wished she could be let off as lightly...

'You were saying...?' Maximilian Grant prompted drily, as if he knew exactly what thoughts were going through her mind.

What had she been saying? Oh, yes... 'I just wanted to explain about what happened earlier this evening—but I realise now there isn't a lot of point to that, is there?' She sighed wearily at the knowledge that it was probably far too late to redeem herself in his eyes.

Would it do any good, she wondered, if she were to tell this man that it hadn't been the defending of *her* honour that had resulted in her ordering Brian to stop the car and let her out, but of his, Maximilian Grant's?

CHAPTER THREE

WELL, not his honour, exactly, but something he valued far more highly: his privacy!

She had been pleased to see Brian earlier when he had joined her and Ally for a drink, had thought him still attractive to her now adult eyes, had been pleased to accept the lift back to Henley Hall he'd offered her once he had realised she was going to leave to catch the last bus back, had even been considering accepting his invitation if he should ask to see her again, for an evening out alone this time. What she had unfortunately forgotten was that Brian now worked for the biggest local newspaper in the area. And what she had learnt during that drive back was that Brian had ambitions to move on from that provincial newspaper to the brighter lights of Fleet Street—or wherever the big national newspapers were located nowadays—and he had the idea of using an exposé of Maximilian Grant's private life to do it, with Sophie as his informant.

At this moment in time, apart from the fact that Maximilian Grant had a sixteen-year-old daughter with a week's half-term holiday to be filled, she knew little or nothing of the man's private life. But, even if she had, she certainly wouldn't have told Brian so that he could write some dreadful story for one of the gory tabloids. She had been outraged that Brian could even have imagined she might!

'There has been a change of plan,' Maximilian Grant gave an abrupt inclination of his head now, the light overhead giving his hair the appearance of being silver

rather than blond, the angles of his face taking on harsh
shadows.

Sophie pulled a face. 'I thought there might have
been,' she grimaced. 'Could you just do me a favour
and go easy on me when you tell Aunt Millie why you
couldn't employ me? She may be your housekeeper, but
she's my mother's sister too, and——'

'I don't think you understand.' He stood up, moving
to sit on the side of the desk. 'The change I spoke of
has nothing to do with this evening——'

'No?' She looked at him with derisive disbelief; who
was he trying to kid? More to the point, why was he
bothering?

'No,' he rasped impatiently. 'The fact is, Jennifer isn't
coming home for the holidays after all, and——'

'I realise you're just saying that to try and save my
feelings,' Sophie shook her head ruefully. 'But I——'

'Miss Gordon, what possible reason could I have for
wanting to save your feelings?' Maximilian Grant looked
down at her, blue eyes mocking.

Indeed. After all, she meant nothing to him, and
neither did her feelings. And he hardly gave the impression of being a man who pulled his punches when
dealing with other people, either verbally or physically.

She could feel the heat enter her cheeks with a slow
burn as he continued to look at her with that pitying
humour that made her feel about the same age as his
daughter!

'Especially if I have to lie to achieve it,' he continued
derisively. 'I deal in facts, Miss Gordon——'

'Sophie,' she put in softly. 'I would rather you called
me Sophie.'

He gave an acknowledging inclination of his head of
the request. 'Well, the facts are—Sophie,' he amended
pointedly, 'that Jennifer is to go to stay with her aunt
for the week instead of coming home. I'm sorry you've

been put to the trouble of coming down here—although, as you said earlier,' his mouth twisted, 'it gave you the opportunity to see your aunt again. And, of course—Brian... wasn't it?' he drawled tauntingly.

'Yes, his name was Brian,' she confirmed in a mutter. 'But we both know how much I could have done without that meeting!'

'Sorry?' Maximilian Grant prompted mockingly as her voice was deliberately pitched too low to be audible to his or anyone else's ears.

'I must say——' She forced a lightness to her voice that she was far from feeling. Given time—she wasn't sure how much time!—she would probably become resigned to the fact that she didn't have a job for the week, after all, but at the moment she just felt completely hollow, not knowing what she was going to do next. But she would bounce back, no doubt about it; she always had in the past. 'I've never actually been sacked before I even started a job before!' It was a first she could have done without now too! Oh, well...

Maximilian Grant's mouth twisted. 'Employers usually wait a little longer than that before dispensing with your services, hmm?' he drawled drily. 'It was your implication, not mine,' he defended at her disgruntled expression.

Given time, she might even have found this man's dry sense of humour amusing—although she doubted it!

'Besides,' he taunted, 'your aunt gave me the impression you haven't quite found your—vocation in life yet... Something about your having tried office work, been a telephonist, done shop work——'

'Yes, OK,' Sophie hastily cut in on what she knew was a long list, although she was sure her aunt would have omitted to mention the kissograms, being a motorbike courier in London, and half a dozen other jobs Aunt Millie wouldn't have considered as suitable refer-

ences for the companion of this man's daughter. She
buried her nose in her coffee-cup so that Maximilian
Grant shouldn't see the possibility of them in her candid
hazel-coloured eyes—because since meeting him she was
sure this man was astute enough to realise exactly the
type of things her aunt had missed out of her résumé!

But he was completely wrong about what she wanted
to do with her life. She knew exactly what she wanted
to do as a career; it was just taking her longer than most
to be in a position to do it. But she would get there in
the end, even if she had to do another two dozen zany
jobs to achieve it.

'Your expenses for coming down here will, of course,
be reimbursed to you.' He stood up now in what was
obviously an end to the conversation, moving to sit
behind the desk again before biting into the sandwich
her aunt had placed there for him. 'Mmm, they're good,'
he said appreciatively after that first bite. 'Try one,' he
invited before continuing to eat.

Food would probably choke her at the moment, her
disappointment over the lack of a job was so acute. 'No,
thanks.' She stood up. 'I—I think I'll go to bed now.
You don't mind if I wait until morning to leave, do you?'
She frowned as that thought occurred to her.

Irritation turned his eyes icy-looking again. 'Don't be
so damned silly,' he rasped angrily. 'If your aunt wants
you to stay on with her for a few days, I'm not going
to object.'

Oh, God . . . Aunt Millie still had to be faced yet! And
no matter what Sophie said to the contrary, her aunt was
sure to assume it must have been something Sophie had
said or done that had influenced Maximilian Grant's decision not to employ her after all, and that her unsuit-
ability reflected on her because she had been the one to
suggest Sophie in the first place! Her aunt wasn't completely responsible for suggesting Sophie anyway;

Sophie's own mother had put the idea to her sister when she had casually mentioned the fact that the family would be here for Jennifer's half-term. And actually, Sophie wasn't totally convinced, despite the fact that this man said otherwise, that her accidental meeting with Maximilian Grant beside the road earlier this evening hadn't influenced his decision concerning her. . .

'I think it's best if I leave tomorrow,' she assured him; there was no point in suffering Aunt Millie's reproachful looks for longer than was necessary.

'As you wish,' he shrugged dismissively, studying some papers that lay on his desktop.

Sophie wondered if he had any idea of the financial blow he had dealt her—even with the reimbursement of her expenses. Probably not. The amount of money she would have earned during the week would have been a mere drop in a very big ocean to this man, but to her. . . Forget it, Sophie, she instructed herself firmly. Move on. Don't look back. Never look back. It was the only way.

Maximilian Grant didn't even seem to notice her leave the room, so engrossed was he in reading those papers and eating his sandwich at the same time. In fact, he had probably already dismissed Sophie Gordon from his mind.

But her aunt Millie hadn't; she was waiting up for her in the kitchen, as Sophie had known she would be!

But to her everlasting relief, when Sophie told her aunt that Jennifer was to go to her aunt's rather than coming home as originally planned, Aunt Millie was so annoyed at the inconsideration shown to her that there was no thought of reproach.

'Well, really!' She stood up to clear the coffee things away. 'But then, I suppose the aunt had a lot to do with that,' she sniffed disapprovingly. 'A spoilt little madam, if ever I saw one. It won't do young Jennifer any good to spend time with that Celia.' She shook her head with foreboding.

Sophie wasn't sure whether it was Jennifer or the aunt who was the spoilt little madam; and she was too relieved at being let off so lightly to want to pursue the subject, excusing herself to go to bed, explaining that she had to travel back to town tomorrow.

'Of course you have.' Her aunt looked guilty now at having delayed her even further. 'And I really am sorry you went to all this trouble just to be disappointed.'

She shrugged. 'Mr Grant said he would pay my expenses——'

'That's the least he could do in the circumstances.' Her aunt still looked disgusted at the way Sophie had been treated.

'Yes,' Sophie grimaced. 'Well. Bed, I think,' she said again firmly.

Aunt Millie nodded, her expression indulgent. 'You have a lie-in in the morning, if you want to. There's no hurry for you to leave,' she added with indignation at the cavalier treatment Sophie had received.

Aunt Millie being so gently kind—especially when Sophie wasn't one hundred per cent certain she deserved it!—was almost as nerve-racking as one of her reprimands could be, Sophie decided, beating a hasty retreat.

But once she reached her bedroom she found she was no longer tired enough to go to bed, her mind racing with alternative plans she could make for the next week. Genteel poverty sounded rather elegant, almost noble, but it didn't pay the bills, or put food in her stomach. Oh, she would find another job, was sure of it, had never failed yet. But until she did...

Maybe if she read for a while she would start to feel sleepy again; the amount of times she had fallen asleep over one of her books in the past, she wouldn't be in the least surprised if it worked now! But the books she had brought with her weren't for light reading, and the more she tried not to think about it, the more the extensive library she had spotted earlier today in the main house seemed to lure her. In fact, one of the first things she had intended doing once she was taken on as Jennifer's companion had been to ask Maximilian Grant if she could have a good look round in there; if—holy of holies!—she might actually be allowed to read some of the leather-bound books if she was very careful with them. Her fingers itched just to touch them.

Maybe Maximilian Grant wouldn't mind if she were to just take a little look in there now...? After all, she wouldn't get another opportunity.

The house, when she ventured out of her bedroom, was in darkness, both her aunt and Maximilian Grant seeming to have gone to bed now. The elegant beauty of the high-ceilinged hallway took on frightening proportions in the shadows of the night, making Sophie wonder if she was really that desperate to have a look in the library after all!

But once she had opened the library door, and literally just smelt all those books, she knew she had to go in and take a look. One of the switches beside the door activated the tall lamp that stood beside the green leather armchair that was placed to one side of the fireplace, the latter filled with a vase of dried flowers this time of year. The central heating was more than adequate for a cool May night.

All the classics were there, all beautifully bound, and, as she had known it would, it gave her pleasure just to touch them.

She didn't believe it, almost the first book she pulled out; *Jane Eyre!* After the thoughts she had had earlier this evening, she knew this was the book she would have to read to get to sleep tonight. Her fingers closed lovingly about the green leather as she pulled the book down from the shelf.

But the book fell to the carpeted floor with a thud as she was grabbed from behind, crying out as her arm was twisted up behind her back and she was spun round in movements so deftly executed that she barely had time to breathe after that first shocked shriek.

And when she found herself pressed up against the hard steel of Maximilian Grant's chest, with wide, frightened eyes staring up into his furiously angry ones, she wasn't sure she was ever going to be able to breathe again!

'You!' he accused her disgustedly, although he made no effort to release her.

When Sophie was becoming more and more desperate by the second that he should do so; she wasn't sure how much longer she was going to be able to remain even standing without breathing!

Close to him like this—very close to him, their bodies moulded together from shoulder to thighs!—she was made aware of every pore of his skin, every harsh line and feature—and at the moment he looked very harsh indeed!—and of the coldness of his eyes, and it was enough to freeze the very blood in her veins. There was certainly no amusement in those eyes now, not even at her expense. In fact, he looked positively hostile!

At the same time as Sophie registered all of this, she also knew that she had never been so aware of a man in her life before. Bone-meltingly, pulse-racingly, cheek-burningly aware of Maximilian Grant with every part of her, her senses singing, from the top of her head to the tips of her tingling toes.

And if she didn't start to breathe again soon she was going to faint dead away at his feet!

Maximilian solved the problem for her by thrusting her away from him, his eyes narrowed to steely slits now as he still held her in his gaze at least. Sophie rubbed at the painful part of her wrist where he had held her so tightly, at the same time taking huge gulps of air into her starved lungs, still too shocked to actually say anything after being taken so much by surprise by the fierceness of his attack.

It must be almost half an hour now since she had left his study, and, while she at least had taken off the uncomfortably high-heeled shoes since going to her bedroom, Maximilian looked exactly as he had when she had left him, still fully clothed and not——

'What are you doing in here?' he demanded harshly, his body tautly challenging.

He looked almost threatening, seeming to bar her way to the door that still stood slightly open, reminding Sophie that she had been the one to leave it that way initially, which was why she hadn't heard Maximilian's entrance a few minutes ago.

She eyed him warily. 'Looking for a book to read...?' She gave a hopeful shrug, wondering why she should have such a strong feeling that he wouldn't believe her; this was the library, after all. What did he think she was doing in here?

The icy-blue gaze didn't waver. 'At this time of the morning?'

He didn't believe her! 'I couldn't sleep after our talk,' she shrugged. 'I mean—I knew I wouldn't be able to, even if I went to bed,' she added hastily as he looked pointedly at the blouse and skirt she still wore, making it obvious that she hadn't even gone to bed to try to sleep yet. 'Too much on my mind,' she grimaced.

He folded his arms in front of his chest. 'A guilty conscience can make you feel like that.'

'Guilty——? Now look here,' she spluttered indignantly. 'I don't have anything to feel guilty about.' She glared at him at the implication that she had. Good God, if he was still going on about her wandering down the darkened road earlier, that had been his fault. And she was going to tell him so too if he didn't stop throwing it up in her face!

Dark blond brows rose over coolly assessing blue eyes. 'Implying that I do?' The query was made silkily soft.

Her gaze dropped from his. 'Well, I certainly have nothing to feel guilty about!' she insisted stubbornly. God, she hadn't been intending to *steal* a book from his precious library, if that were what he was worried about; could she do nothing right where this man was concerned? 'I realise that perhaps I should have asked before borrowing a book.' Her gaze returned the challenge in his now. 'But given the lateness of the hour, and the fact that I would have returned the book to its shelf in the morning before I left, without anyone being any the wiser——' she watched as he bent down to retrieve the book from the carpeted floor at their feet '—I didn't think that would be necessary. Obviously I was wrong,' she added tautly.

He turned the book over in his hands that were long and slender, but nevertheless gave the impression of a steely strength. Sophie knew just how strong they could be, could still feel the imprint of those artistically shaped fingers on her wrist. She was trying hard not to remember how being hauled unceremoniously up against him had affected her. Luckily, his insulting behaviour since was making that very easy to do!

'*Jane Eyre.*' His mouth twisted mockingly as he read the title printed in gold-leaf on the front and spine of the book. 'Let me guess,' he derided harshly. 'The arrogant but wealthy Rochester is a hero of yours?'

Sophie could cheerfully have slapped him at that moment for the cynical insult in his voice. In fact, she had to clasp her hands behind her back to stop herself from doing just that; she felt at that moment that she preferred Maximilian Grant cynically suspicious rather than derisively mocking! 'Luckily,' she snapped, 'Rochester has more than his wealth to endear him to Jane; he is also blessed with a sense of humour!'

Maximilian's mouth twisted, the implication not lost on him. 'And you think I'm not?'

Sophie's head tilted back challengingly, red curls gleaming like flame. 'From our acquaintance so far, I wouldn't know!'

He laughed at her sharp retort, actually laughed, while putting the book down on the coffee-table that stood beside the armchair. 'Perhaps it's a pity you won't be staying on here after all, Sophie Gordon,' he murmured softly, still smiling. 'It seems I'm in need of reminding how to laugh at situations.'

Sophie was so mesmerised by the transformation the laughter had effected in the harshness of his features—the eyes a deep blue with humour, laughter-lines appearing beside his nose and mouth, his teeth very white and even against his tanned skin—that initially she didn't take in what he had said. And then, when she did, she could only reflect how sad it must be to have to be reminded how to laugh.

What sort of life did this man lead, that he should need reminding? She knew he was a widower, her aunt had told her that, but from what she could gather his wife had died three years ago, so surely there must be another love in his life by this time, someone who could share in his laughter? It wasn't very likely, Sophie was sure, that a physically fit man of thirty-nine should have remained celibate since the death of his wife, not when he had the added bonus of looking the way Maximilian Grant did. But she mustn't think about how attractive he was, certainly shouldn't remember that fierce physical ache she had known when her body was pressed so intimately against his such a short time ago!

And there was his daughter, sixteen-year-old Jennifer; didn't she bring laughter and happiness into his life? As lovingly close to her own parents as she was, she couldn't see how a father and daughter left alone together couldn't become even closer because of their loss. But perhaps Maximilian Grant's wealth even put a barrier between himself and his daughter; it would be extremely difficult in such circumstances, and given Maximilian's wealth, not to at least financially spoil a young girl who had been left motherless. Perhaps there was something to be said for genteel poverty, after all...

'Now, it seems, I've taken the laughter from your life too,' Maximilian murmured with regret, blue eyes narrowed as he watched the differing emotions flickering across her face.

'Oh, no,' she hastened to reassure him. 'I was just—thinking,' she told him lamely, hoping he wouldn't ask what she had been thinking about; she doubted that people very often felt sorry for this man, or that he would thank them for doing it!

'A dangerous pastime, I've found,' he drawled dismissively. 'I think it's time we went to bed now, don't you? Why, "Jane",' he taunted as her face went pink. 'You surely didn't think I was suggesting we go to bed *together*?' He raised his brows mockingly.

This man did have a sense of humour after all, even if it was a little cruel! 'Of course not,' she snapped. 'Mr Rochester would never have suggested anything so improper,' she mocked in return.

Maximillian's mouth twisted. 'A twentieth-century Rochester might,' he said softly. 'Remember, *he* wasn't averse to trying to marry Jane while already having a wife!'

Sophie gave that some thought. Mr Rochester hadn't been above trying to take what he wanted, namely Jane as his wife, any way that he could within the bounds of

Jane's propriety; a modern-day Rochester probably *would* use complete seduction to achieve the same end!

'How lucky for both of us, then, that you aren't Mr Rochester or I Jane,' she dismissed lightly.

That piercing blue gaze held her steady hazel-coloured one for several seconds before he gave a slow inclination of his head, his hair looking silver in the lamplight. 'How lucky for us both,' he echoed softly. 'Take your book now, Sophie, and go.'

She didn't even rise indignantly to the order as she would normally have done; she hastily picked up the book from the table—although she was no longer sure she wanted to read it!—and hurried over to the door. She hesitated when she reached it, turning back to look at him. He stood completely still, staring into the unlit fireplace, a man alone—and strangely lonely... No! If Maximilian Grant was alone—*or* lonely—it was because he chose to be that way, and for no other reason. Sophie hurried from the library before any more doubts about the truth of that could take root and grow.

What a strange, strange evening... She couldn't ever remember another like it. And her response to Maximilian's closeness had come as a complete shock to her. Oh, he was ruggedly handsome in that harshly autocratic way, but hardly her type, surely? And yet... Held so tightly against him, pressed to the hardness of his body, their differences in age, experience, hadn't seemed to matter—in fact, she hadn't given them a thought! At that moment, with Maximilian's face so close to her own, her gaze transfixed by his, she had just wanted him to kiss her!

It was the oddest feeling, then, when it seemed only minutes since she had finally drifted off to sleep after hours of lying awake tormented by that realisation, to awaken with the certain knowledge that there was someone moving stealthily about her bedroom...!

CHAPTER FOUR

SOPHIE had been having the strangest dream—involving telephones and women locked away in attics!—that it took her several seconds to realise she was actually awake, and that she wasn't alone in her bedroom!

It was difficult to make out who it was, with the curtains pulled across the windows and throwing the room into shadow, but as her eyes became accustomed to the gloom she could see a figure standing over by the dressing-table, could—my God, she could hear the sound of coins jingling together. Her money. That she had placed on top of the dressing-table before going to bed. All the money she possessed in the world!

Maximilian might have briefly thought last night, when he first came across her in the library, that she was a burglar, but it seemed she now—incredibly!—had a genuine one! And she didn't know what to do, what—

'Oh, you're awake, are you?' drawled a light feminine voice scathingly. 'I thought perhaps you were going to sleep the whole day away!'

Sophie wasn't sure how she had given herself away—perhaps an involuntary movement, or a change in the tenor of her breathing; but even as she struggled up into a sitting position the figure across the room moved towards the window and whipped back the curtains.

Blinding sunlight blazed into the room, and for a moment Sophie was too dazzled to see anything but that bright light. And then, as her eyes became accustomed to the sunlight, she was at last able to see what her intruder looked like.

And she didn't look much like an intruder at all, more like Alice in Wonderland, with her long cascade of golden hair secured back from her face with a black band, her face that of a blue-eyed angel, the blue and white checked dress she wore secured at her slender waist with a narrow white belt. In fact, the way she looked, and the dress she was wearing, seemed a little young for her height, for she was easily taller than Sophie despite her apparent youth.

The young girl stood beside the bed looking down at Sophie now, her top lip curled back disdainfully. 'I thought I would come and see what a *paid* companion actually looked like!' she dismissed with obvious contempt for the role.

And obviously not an angel, after all, in spite of the way she looked!

On closer inspection, the eyes were a familiar icy blue, the small pointed chin set at a determined angle. The outward shows of Maximilian Grant's strength of character were certainly far from attractive on his sixteen-year-old daughter—because Sophie didn't doubt now that this was who her 'intruder' was!

'You aren't supposed to be here.' Sophie frowned, getting out of bed, aware as she did so that Jennifer was watching her every move, critically assessing, no doubt, the exact cost of the mass-produced chain-store cream nightshirt that Sophie was wearing, which although it had a silky look and feel to it, most certainly wasn't something as extravagant as silk.

It was disconcerting to be looked at so scathingly by one so young. And it wasn't difficult now to see why Maximilian's daughter didn't share laughter with him; this young lady took herself far too seriously for that!

'It's all there,' Jennifer scorned. 'Your money,' she explained derisively as Sophie turned to her questioningly. 'I was only counting how much was there, not attempting to take any of it.' She moved to sit on the bed—well, fall on it actually, with little regard for its safety, looking up at Sophie challengingly. 'Is that all the money you have with you?' She arched dark blonde brows in a way that was all too reminiscent of her father.

Sophie glanced across at the two crumpled five-pound notes and the pile of change that came to exactly fifty-six pence; she knew, because she had carefully counted it the night before! It was all the money she had in the world, not just with her. 'As a matter of fact, yes.' She shrugged dismissively.

Jennifer gave a disgusted snort. "Then no wonder you don't mind being a paid companion to someone you've never even met; Daddy gives me more than that as a weekly allowance!'

That wasn't difficult to believe, but what this young lady really needed was a smacked bottom! 'Perhaps that's one of the reasons your father needs to pay someone to be your companion,' she returned softly.

For a brief moment the insult seemed to have gone over Jennifer's snooty young head, and then her eyes widened indignantly. 'I beg your pardon . . . ?'

'That's perfectly all right.' Sophie smiled at her disarmingly, deliberately misunderstanding her. 'I'm sure you didn't mean to be rude.'

The young girl flushed, standing up now, her hands clenched at her sides. 'Well, that's where you're wrong; I meant to be very rude indeed!'

Jennifer would be stamping her foot with frustrated anger in a moment, Sophie surmised with amusement, wondering how often such a display, a display Maximilian Grant would abhor, had managed to get Jennifer her own way in the past.

'Then you succeeded, didn't you?' she dismissed pleasantly before taking her hairbrush from her bag and turning her back on the young girl, to look at her own reflection in the mirror and begin the morning ritual of taming her fiery locks; after a vigorous brushing they might fall into some sort of order.

But she could see Jennifer's reflection behind her too, knew the young girl was momentarily thrown off balance by her reaction to her deliberate rudeness. Sophie couldn't even begin to guess at the reasons for the rudeness, but she did remember herself what it was like to be sixteen, and she could at least sympathise with the sheer frustration of being treated as that child-woman, too old to be made the allowances people would a child, but yet too young still to be treated as an adult. And it obviously rankled deeply with the young girl that her father had deemed it necessary to employ someone to spend time with her during her half-term holiday from school.

But that didn't answer the question as to what Jennifer was doing here at all, when only last night Maximilian had told her his daughter wouldn't be coming home for the holiday after all, but spending it at her aunt's house. Unless he *had* lied to her? But Sophie didn't think that was the case either. She had believed him—arrogant as he was!—when he told her he certainly wouldn't stoop to lying to stop her feelings being hurt; Maximilian Grant would always be brutally honest, she was sure of it. But it...

'My God!' she gasped, having caught the reflection of her wrist-watch in the mirror and seen that it was almost one o'clock. Lunchtime! Jennifer's initial comment about her 'sleeping the whole day away' now made complete sense.

She had had no idea it was so late. Of course, it had been almost three o'clock in the morning before she finally climbed into bed and fell asleep, but even so...!

'Someone should have woken me.' She frowned, wondering what on earth Maximilian Grant must think of her sleeping in until this time. She didn't doubt that he had been up for hours, despite his own lack of sleep the night before; he looked the type who only needed a couple of hours' rest a night to be able to get up fresh and alert the next day!

'*Someone* did,' Jennifer drawled, her brows raised pointedly.

God, yes. 'Did your father send you?' Sophie asked as she reached inside the wardrobe for her bag, putting it on to the bed to begin putting her things inside.

'No, he—what are you doing?' Jennifer frowned as she watched her hurried movements.

'Packing, of course,' Sophie told her impatiently, leaving out on the bed the denims and red T-shirt she intended wearing for the day, and putting everything else inside the holdall. 'Didn't your father tell you that he had changed his mind about the "paid companion"?' she dismissed distractedly, looking about the room to make sure there was nothing she had forgotten; she always travelled light, but what she did take was always a necessity.

Jennifer still frowned. 'I haven't actually spoken to my father yet.'

'What?' Sophie came to a skidding halt on her way to the bathroom to wash and dress before leaving, staring at the young girl disbelievingly.

Jennifer returned the gaze defiantly. 'My father has no idea yet that I'm even here,' she announced haughtily, although that arrogance was belied slightly by a flicker of uncertainty in the blue of her eyes. 'I took a taxi home from school,' she added challengingly.

It must be some allowance, to have covered the cost of that taxi fare! It also explained the way Jennifer was dressed; the blue and white checked dress was obviously her school's summer uniform. But if Maximilian Grant didn't even know his daughter was at home...!

'Don't you think you ought to have at least said hello to your father as soon as you got home?' Sophie suggested slowly, wondering what Maximilian Grant was going to have to say at having his plans changed so arbitrarily by this sixteen-year-old female version of himself!

Jennifer, for all her defiance, was obviously wondering the same thing, plucking nervously, with long, elegant fingers, at the belt on her dress. 'I'm in no hurry for the explosion I know is sure to follow.' She shrugged with a knowing grimace. 'But I also have no intention of being foisted off on my aunt Celia for the week either!' she added rebelliously.

Sophie came fully back into the bedroom, frowning heavily. She had a feeling Jennifer was going to be proved correct about the explosion; she couldn't somehow see Maximilian Grant taking his daughter's disobedience lightly. And she couldn't exactly blame him... 'But can't you see he might already be worried about you?' she reasoned. 'He may have already rung his sister to speak to you, or she may have rung him when you didn't arrive at her home as expected. Or——'

'Aunt Celia isn't *Daddy's* sister!' Jennifer cut in scathingly. 'She's *Mummy's* younger sister,' she explained with dislike. 'And she only offered to let me go to her house at all this week because she has the hots for Daddy——'

'Jennifer!' Sophie gasped, not able to allow this disrespect to pass unchecked.

'I hate being called Jennifer!' the young girl snapped aggressively. 'Jen, or Jennie, but never Jennifer.'

'All right—Jennie.' Sophie shrugged, dismissing the importance of what name she called the young girl by when there was something so much more important to discuss. Although...she couldn't help wondering if Maximilian Grant returned the 'hots' for the young sister of his dead wife! 'Being insulting about your aunt doesn't alter the fact that once your father discovers you haven't arrived at her house as arranged, he's going to be very worried——'

'It certainly doesn't!' rasped a coldly forbidding voice.

Both girls had spun round towards the open doorway at the first sound of that harshly angry voice, Jennie initially with guilt, though this was quickly followed by a return of that defiance, Sophie self-consciously, wondering just how much of their conversation he had overheard, and then becoming aware of how scantily dressed she was for this meeting with him, wearing nothing beneath the nightshirt.

Colour slowly warmed her cheeks at the realisation, her nipples, as if fully aware of her predicament, choosing that moment to harden beneath the soft material, thrusting proudly forward.

Not that Maximilian Grant looked in any mood at that moment to notice whether she was fully clothed or completely naked; his furious attention was firmly fixed on his daughter! Nevertheless, Sophie clutched her clothes in front of her defensively.

'Do you have any idea of the trouble that's been caused by your thoughtless behaviour, young lady?' Maximilian Grant attacked savagely. 'The police have been informed of your disappearance——'

'The police...?' Jennie echoed dazedly, her cheeks paling, her eyes a haunted blue.

'Of course,' her father rasped, striding fully into the room, looking as Sophie had known he would—fresh and alert, in dark fitted trousers and another one of those white silk shirts he favoured, even though he could have got to bed no earlier than her; in fact, it might have been much later, for he had still been in the library when she went to her room.

Jennie gaped at her father. 'But——'

'What else did you expect me to do when I had telephoned Celia and she said you hadn't arrived there, and yet the school claimed you had left there over two hours ago?' her father pointed out exasperatedly. 'I thought I was going insane when after all that I heard the sound of your voice here!' He shook his head dazedly; the relief of finding that his daughter was safe after all was still over-shadowed by the angry realisation of just how unnecessary his worry had been in the first place!

Jennie swallowed hard, and although Sophie knew that the young girl's behaviour had been selfishly inconsiderate, at the same time she couldn't help admiring the way Jennie refused to back down even before her father's obvious anger at her actions. Given half a chance, and if her determination to have her own way could be curbed a little, Jennie Grant might even become a passably likeable human being!

'I was just introducing myself to—to——' Jennie looked at a loss suddenly as she realised that, although she had very forcefully informed Sophie what name she preferred to be known by, she actually had no idea of Sophie's own name!

'Sophie,' she put in helpfully, beginning to feel a little sorry for the other girl; she certainly wouldn't want, after her own run-in with Maximilian Grant the night before, to be in Jennie's shoes during the next ten minutes or so!

'It would seem you and Miss Gordon hadn't progressed too far in this so-called introduction,' Jennie's father derided harshly. 'And now I would suggest the two of us leave her in privacy so that she can at least put some clothes on!'

She had been wrong; this man had noted exactly what she was, or *wasn't*, wearing!

Her cheeks coloured anew as she realised he had probably been fully aware of the betrayal of her body seconds ago, too. God, she was excelling even herself in embarrassing moments with this man as witness! Poor Aunt Millie, although she had no idea of it, would have a lot to live down over the next few weeks!

Jennie, who had shown herself to be rebellious, certainly *wasn't* stupid, for she preceded her father to the door, not even sparing Sophie a second glance as she did so. Not that Sophie could exactly blame her; the poor girl must feel as if she were on her way to the gallows!

Maximilian Grant didn't immediately follow his daughter from the bedroom; his gaze levelled on the packed bag on the bed before returning to Sophie. 'Don't leave until I've spoken to you again,' he rasped abruptly, following Jennie out into the carpeted hallway now, and closing the bedroom door firmly behind him.

Sophie dropped down weakly on to the unmade bed, feeling as if she had just been put through an emotional wringer. She wasn't one of those people who woke up all bright and cheerful—even at lunchtime! She needed time and space to prepare herself for the day ahead; the Grant family seemed to meet life head-on, no matter what time of day it was!

And what had that last remark of Maximilian Grant's meant? Did he mean not to leave until he'd had a chance to reprimand her for her part in his not being told immediately of his daughter's presence here, or did he mean something else entirely? Whatever, it was prudent not to go anywhere until he had at least finished talking to Jennie about her selfishly thoughtless actions.

Her aunt was in the middle of preparing what was obviously going to be a late lunch when Sophie joined her in the kitchen a short time later. Jennie's behaviour seemed to have affected the whole household. But there was a fresh pot of coffee ready on the percolator, and so Sophie poured herself a cup, sipping it gratefully. She still didn't feel one hundred percent in tune with the world yet, even if she had luxuriated in a hot shower before dressing, her riotous curls now combed into some sort of order.

Her aunt gave her a knowing look as she turned and saw her. 'I can't say I'm exactly surprised young Jennifer took it into her head to make her own arrangements for the holiday,' she said with rueful satisfaction. 'As strong-willed as her father, that one.' She shook her head. 'Still, it's lucky for you, isn't it?' She poured the remaining coffee into a china coffee-pot before putting it on a tray that was already laid up with a cup, sugar, and cream.

Sophie frowned, not seeing the significance at all, but then she wasn't thinking properly yet. 'Is it?'

'Well, of course it is.' Her aunt gave her an impatient look for being so obtuse. 'You can have your job now that Jennifer has come home after all.' She picked up the laden tray. 'Take this through to the library, will you, while I carry on with lunch?' She turned away distractedly.

Sophie didn't move. Maybe she had missed something in the conversation, but she didn't for one moment believe that, just because Jennie was here now, *she* was actually going to remain here. Father and daughter might both be strong-willed, but Sophie didn't doubt which one was the stronger!

'Take the tray through to the library, Sophie,' her aunt reminded her impatiently when she turned round and found her still standing there with the tray in her hands. 'Before the coffee gets cold,' she added pointedly.

Sophie went. She needed to go to the library before she left, anyway, to return the book she had borrowed the night before. Besides, it would be interesting to see just how father and daughter were getting on now; they had ordered coffee, so they couldn't still be at each other's throats.

To her puzzlement the library appeared empty when she entered after the briefest of taps with the toe of her shoe, and she put the tray down on the coffee-table with a frown. She had expected to at least hear voices in the room, if not actual shouting; certainly she hadn't expected that there would be no one here at all!

'Thanks,' a deep voice murmured appreciatively.

Sophie spun round with a startled gasp, just in time to see a man getting up from the depths of the green leather wing-backed chair that faced towards the fireplace. She hadn't noticed him sitting there when she came in, the chair back slightly towards her, but as he stood up fully she realised he wasn't the man she had been expecting to find in here anyway. This man was younger than Maximilian Grant, probably in his early thirties, with dark hair cut severely short, his eyes brown, in an attractive face that somehow seemed to lack humour, his dark suit as austere as the rest of him.

'Did I startle you?' he apologised lightly. 'I didn't mean to, I was just thanking you for bringing my coffee.' He looked pointedly at the tray she had just put down.

'*Your* coffee...?' She had assumed that the tray was for Maximilian Grant and Jennie, although, now that she thought about it, her aunt hadn't actually said that it was.

The man grimaced. 'Max is still talking to Jennie in his study. And you would be...?' He quirked dark brows curiously.

In the study. Of course. It was the place Maximilian seemed to choose for unpleasant interviews!

'Sophie Gordon.' She held her hand out to the man politely.

'Paul Wiseman.' He returned the gesture, his hand strong and firm. 'I'm Mr Grant's assistant. I drove down this morning to join him here.'

Ah, that explained a lot. At least...she thought it did. If Maximilian had been going to work down here for at least this weekend anyway, why had he arranged for Jennie to go to her aunt?

'That's nice,' she said inanely, releasing her hand.

His brows rose again. 'Is it?'

Sophie gave a rueful smile. 'To tell you the truth, I don't actually know!' she confided. 'I was to work for Mr Grant too, but it didn't work out,' she dismissed with a shrug, realising even as she did so that she was perhaps confiding too much to this man; he was probably Maximilian Grant's friend as well as his assistant.

Paul Wiseman's attention seemed to sharpen at that. 'Oh, yes?'

Was it her imagination—was she just too sensitive to the situation here—or did this man suddenly seem wary too? 'Don't worry.' She gave a dismissive laugh. 'I wasn't after your job! Nothing so grand.' She grimaced. 'Child companion is about my limit at the moment. Although Jennie is far from being a child.' She pulled a rueful face at the memory of the self-possessed young lady who had invaded her bedroom earlier.

'At the moment?' Paul Wiseman repeated curiously.

Sophie frowned at the way he homed in on that part of her conversation, trying very hard to dismiss the feelings of irritation this man gave her. After all, she didn't even know him. But it was just very disconcerting the way he seemed to ask her questions without actually giving much away about himself, only his name and that he worked for Maximilian Grant and that he had driven down here this morning to join him. And that still rankled with Sophie too, if she was honest; Maximilian Grant had all the rest of his time to work, day and night if he chose to, so surely it wasn't too much to ask for him to spend some time with his daughter during her school holidays? If that was the case, then she couldn't actually blame Jennie for taking matters into her own hands and deciding for herself where she wanted to spend the week!

Consequently her own reply to Paul Wiseman's probing was sharper than it might otherwise have been. 'It's human nature to want to better oneself. I don't intend spending all my time as a part-time student and filling in with an assortment of jobs at the same time!'

Paul looked at her searchingly. 'Part-time student?' he echoed softly. 'Of what?'

This man had no right having brown eyes that should have been warm and friendly, when he was almost as sharp as his employer! She had told him far too much about herself already, and she had no intention of telling him any more, especially when it must be obvious that she was a little old to be a student. But she had made some wrong decisions in her life, and now she was having to work twice as hard to regain the ground she had lost.

'Of life, Mr Wiseman,' she dismissed with what she was well aware was facetious evasion of his question.

'We're all students of that, Sophie,' he murmured softly, his probing gaze still fixed on her slightly flushed face with its intriguing smattering of freckles across her nose and cheeks. 'I had the feeling that you were referring to something more specific?'

She frowned at his persistence. She had never exactly made a secret of the fact that she was working feverishly on an Open University course, but she didn't go around boring everyone with it either, mainly because they then wanted to know why she didn't just go to university as a full-time student. As this man obviously did. And his continued curiosity about her was irritating her intensely!

'Did you?' she dismissed brightly. 'I'd better go, Mr Wiseman, I have to catch a train back to London this afternoon.' She turned to leave, aware as she did so that he was still watching her with that annoying intensity. She had no doubt that he made Maximilian Grant a good assistant, but as far as Sophie was concerned he was almost as rude as his employer! Almost...

If she kept telling herself how rude and disagreeable Maximilian Grant was, she might even manage to forget her attraction to him the night before! Not that there had been any memory, in the harshness of his face earlier, of that physical closeness they had shared last night, although, to give him his due, at the time he had been worried and then angry at Jennie's thoughtless behaviour. He hadn't exactly——

'Did you want to leave the book, Sophie?' Paul Wiseman spoke softly from just behind her.

In fact, he was so close behind her, when she turned, that she instantly took an involuntary step backwards, glaring up at him accusingly for making her feel that she had to do such a thing.

'I assumed,' he spoke derisively, 'as you have a book under your arm which belongs to the set in the library, that you were probably wanting to return it before you left.' He looked at her pointedly.

The book, *Jane Eyre*; she had completely forgotten, during her conversation with this man, that she had put it under her arm so that she could carry both it and the tray into the library earlier. And she certainly hadn't had the memory-lapse because of any enjoyment of her conversation with this man; on the contrary, he had agitated her so much that she had simply forgotten the book altogether. A book she was rapidly going off anyway; the damned thing seeming to have caused her nothing but trouble since she had first spotted it—mainly because the men in this house all seemed to think she was trying to steal it!

'Of course,' she snapped, putting the book back in the appropriate space on the shelf. 'Goodbye, Mr Wiseman,' she added pointedly as she went to the door once again.

'Do you think so?' he returned with his first show of amusement so far.

She frowned at the enigmatic remark. 'Mr Wiseman, it's been a very unsettling——'

'Call me Paul, please,' he invited smoothly. 'The informality makes for a more harmonious working relationship.' He shrugged dismissively.

And, as the two of them wouldn't be working together, it wasn't relevant! Now that she had made his acquaintance, as well as Maximilian Grant's, she was beginning to wonder why she had ever been upset that this job had fallen through. Coupled with Jennie Grant herself, this job would have been a hard haul at best; at its worst it would have been downright impossible!

She gave him a bright, meaningless smile before turning to leave once again, wondering if he had actually listened to any of the replies she had made to his nosy questioning—only to walk straight into the solid wall of a chest she was beginning to recognise only too well! And if she hadn't been familiar with what it felt like to be crushed against Maximilian Grant's chest like this, she would have recognised that crisp, tangy aftershave he wore anyway, its smell heady to her senses.

'We'll have to stop meeting like this,' he murmured huskily as she put a hand up on his chest to steady herself, looking down at her with darkened eyes, those same eyes moving questioningly as he saw a movement slightly behind her, his arms slowly dropping from about her waist as he recognised Paul Wiseman. 'Paul,' he greeted abruptly, his gaze guarded now. 'The two of you have introduced yourselves?' he prompted harshly, looking from Sophie's flushed face across to Paul Wiseman's enigmatic one, and then back again.

Sophie's blush deepened under that narrow-eyed stare. What was he looking at her like that for? He surely didn't think... Good God, the man was his employee, and just because Maximilian believed he had found her in a compromising

situation with Brian last night, there was no reason to believe she made a habit of flirting with every man she came into contact with!

But what of the fact that she had been in Maximilian's own arms last night, too...?

That was different, she inwardly defended herself indignantly, and was certainly no reason for——

'Sophie brought our coffee in for us, Mr Grant,' Paul Wiseman was the one to answer him dismissively.

And formally. So much for his claim of informality making for 'a more harmonious working relationship'; it certainly didn't apply to his own relationship with Maximilian Grant! Paul Wiseman was a fraud. Unless he had actually been flirting with her when he'd made that remark...? If he had, she hated to disappoint him, but she found him as attractive as a cold kipper!

It was ridiculous, really; for the last couple of years she had avoided men completely, and now within the space of twenty-four hours she had been in the company of three more than presentable men all in one go. One who had tried to charm her into betraying confidences she hadn't even been privileged to—and now was never likely to be!—a second man who had assumed the very worst about her relationship with the first man and had treated her accordingly, and now a third man who seemed to be watching her and Maximilian very closely! Three men—and she wanted nothing more to do with any of them.

Maximilian nodded abruptly. 'Your aunt told me you had come in here, Sophie,' he spoke to her curtly. 'I wanted to talk to you,' he explained.

The sooner they got this conversation over with, the better as far as Sophie was concerned. She just wanted to get back to London as soon as possible and start looking for another job for the week. She couldn't get away from here fast enough!

She nodded. 'I thought I might as well help my aunt out while I was waiting for you to finish your discussion with Jennie,' she said dismissively.

He glanced briefly across at Paul Wiseman. 'My study, I think,' he told Sophie with his usual arrogance. 'Go ahead and have your coffee, Paul,' he invited smoothly. 'I should be finished here soon, and then we can get down to discussing things properly.'

Sophie preceded him from the room only because it was obvious that was what she was expected to do. 'Finished here' obviously meant he was going to pay her the expenses he had promised and then send her on her way; she felt like an unwanted parcel he had to dispose of. A sub-standard one at that!

Jennie was no longer in Maximilian's study when they got to the room, and Sophie couldn't help feeling sorry for the young girl all over again as she guessed, from Maximilian's grim expression as he sat down behind the desk, that what had taken place in this study a short time ago hadn't been pleasant—for either of them. At the same time as she knew that, Sophie had no doubt who had been the victor. Poor Jennie might already have been packed off to the aunt who 'had the hots' for Maximilian!

Did Maximilian 'have the hots' for 'Aunt Celia' too? Was that the reason he was so determined Jennie would go there? Looking at him now, blue eyes glacial, his mouth a thin, uncompromising line, Sophie couldn't imagine this man wildly in love, or even wildly passionate, about any woman.

And yet...she recalled with a slight fluttering of her own pulse, there had been an attraction between them last night that...

'—forgot to ask your aunt if you can ride,' Maximilian was saying impatiently. 'I hope you do, because Jennifer is upstairs changing into her riding things right now, and I would hate to disappoint her by telling her she isn't going, which she isn't if you can't accompany her,' he said with finality.

Sophie stared at him uncomprehendingly. Jennie was upstairs changing into her riding clothes...? He wanted *Sophie* to go *where* with her...?

'But—but I thought——' She shook her head, frowning her puzzlement.

'Yes?' he challenged harshly, eyes as hard as flint— and almost the same colour! 'Just exactly what did you "think", Miss Gordon?'

Whatever it was, the mood he was in, she wasn't stupid enough to actually voice it! He obviously hadn't emerged the victor at all. And from his mood now it was obvious he didn't take defeat gracefully, was almost daring her now to remind him that Jennie—Sophie had noticed that Maximilian called his daughter by her full name, something she had professed to hate—shouldn't be staying on here at all but going to her aunt's house. Sophie had no intention of making such a mistake, was sure his outward calm was just that, that inside he probably felt like strangling someone. And Sophie wasn't putting herself up as a likely candidate!

'Jenni-fer——' she remembered just in time to use the young girl's full name, not sure yet whether it was just Maximilian's anger with his daughter that was making him use her full name, or if he just didn't like it being shortened '—wants to go riding?' she queried brightly.

He nodded tersely. 'Right now. So, if you still want the job, I suggest you go and keep her company.'

Now. He might be 'suggesting' it, but she was left in no doubt that it was really an order to be obeyed!

Sophie obeyed. Without argument or question. Forgetting completely, as she did so, that a few minutes ago she had been determined to get away from here...

CHAPTER FIVE

IF MAXIMILIAN GRANT didn't have the look of the victor, then neither did Jennie, her expression petulant as she fastened the last button on her dark green riding jacket before slamming shut her wardrobe door and turning from looking at her reflection in the full-length mirror on the door to glare at Sophie as she stood in the open doorway.

Sophie had stopped off in the kitchen just long enough to tell her aunt she was staying after all, before hurrying up to the bedroom she knew was Jennie's. The door had been left open, and it only needed the briefest of glimpses inside to tell her Jennie was not a very tidy young lady; she had only been back in the house a very short time, and yet already there were clothes strewn all over the bedroom. Although, as she turned to Sophie with that angry glitter of challenge in her icy blue eyes, Sophie wasn't at all sure that wasn't due to sheer temper rather than a genuine untidiness!

'Come to gloat, have you?' she snapped resentfully, securing her hair back at her nape with a black ribbon as she spoke, her movements sure and capable.

Sophie wasn't sure... but she didn't think so. What exactly did she have to gloat about? Surely Jennie was the one who had got her own way? But to reveal to the young girl that she didn't even know what she was talking about would instantly put her at a disadvantage, and with this self-possessed young lady she already knew she needed every ounce of calm assurance she had at her disposal!

'Not really,' she dismissed non-committally, her smile one of open friendliness.

Jennie gave her a scathing glance, snatching her riding hat up off the bed. 'I suppose you have to earn a living somehow.' She was deliberately insulting, her top lip turned back contemptuously. 'But I'm sure there has to be a better way for you to do it than being my gaoler!'

Sophie's eyes widened at the accusation. She had imagined—before she met Jennie—that the two of them could become friends, have fun together, go shopping, for long walks, have trips into town to the cinema and small theatre there, and even now she had realised Jennie wasn't the young girl eager for her company that she had been hoping for she had still hoped they might manage to salvage something of the week they were to spend together. But if this was the way Jennie was going to look on even having her here...

'Maybe I should tell your father this isn't such a good idea after all,' she suggested ruefully. 'I had hoped we might be friends——'

'Friends!' Jennie spat the word out incredulously, her eyes flashing angrily. 'I either agree to have you here as my companion or I have to go to Aunt Celia's after all; what sort of basis would you call that for friendship?'

So that was Maximilian Grant's condition for allowing Jennie to stay here after all! Didn't he realise that by doing it that way he was making her position here almost impossible from the outset? 'Jennie——'

'Are you his latest mistress—is that it?' Jennie's eyes were narrowed challengingly as the idea occurred to her. 'Is that the reason he's so determined to keep you here?'

Sophie couldn't help wincing at the deliberate insult in the young girl's tone and expression. And she didn't doubt for one moment that she was meant to feel very insulted indeed. Just as she couldn't exactly blame Jennie for feeling this burning resentment towards her if her father really had given her such an ultimatum about staying here. And maybe Jennie had some past experience from which to base her accusation on...?

'You don't actually believe that yourself, Jennie,' she told the other girl crisply. 'No, you don't,' she insisted ruefully as Jennie would have protested. 'And I'm really sorry your father chose to put things to you in the way that he did. I think the best thing for all of us is if I just explain to your father that my staying here just wouldn't work out, and leave it at that, don't you?' she encouraged without rancour.

Jennie's gaze narrowed suspiciously. 'You would actually do that?' she said slowly.

'Of course,' Sophie confirmed without hesitation.

'But it means you would be out of a job,' Jennie reminded, still wary.

'Of course I'd rather stay here and have the job,' she acknowledged ruefully. 'But——'

'Then it looks as if we're stuck with each other, doesn't it,' Jennie drawled dismissively. 'Because I have no intention of going to Aunt—— Why, speak of the...' Her attention was caught and held by what she had seen out of the window.

Or rather *who*, Sophie realised, gravitating over towards the window herself, standing next to Jennie now as the two of them looked down on to the driveway, Jennie's bedroom having a view out of the front of the house.

There were three cars parked in the forecourt now, Maximilian's sleek green BMW, a silver-coloured Rover that Sophie assumed had to belong to Paul Wiseman, and parked next to this was a sporty white Mercedes; climbing out from behind the wheel of the latter was one of the most beautiful women Sophie had ever seen!

Tall, and elegantly dressed, in a short body-hugging purple dress, hair as black as coal falling silkily down to her shoulders, the woman was lovely enough to be a photographic model, or even a film star, her skin tanned a beautiful golden brown, her legs long, bare and shapely as she walked towards the house on high-heeled shoes that perfectly matched the colour of her dress.

'She didn't waste any time, did she?' Jennie scorned, giving Sophie a derisive look as she still looked puzzled. 'My dear aunt Celia,' Jennie explained mockingly, 'come to pay us a call. So if you do have any designs on Daddy, I should go downstairs now and protect your interest!'

That was 'Aunt Celia'? Sophie could no longer actually see the other woman, she had moved into the entry porch now, but her image was very vivid in her memory; Celia didn't look like anyone's aunt, sexual magnetism oozing out of every pore as she moved so gracefully.

But what intrigued Sophie even more than the way the other woman looked was that she had managed to arrive here so quickly after informing Maximilian that Jennie hadn't arrived at her house as they had planned; just where was her house, that she could get here this quickly?

But Sophie knew she had to deal with Jennie's last taunt before settling any curiosity about the beautiful woman who had just arrived. 'I believe we were going riding?' she prompted pointedly.

Jennie returned her gaze steadily for several minutes, and then she gave a slow nod. 'So we were,' she accepted knowingly, moving across the room towards the door now. 'Let's escape now, before I get dragged downstairs and forced to apologise to Aunt Celia.' She stopped in the doorway, glancing back impatiently. 'Sophie!' she prompted irritably when she saw she hadn't moved. 'If we get out now, Celia will be left a clear run to charm Daddy. Which will put her in a good mood.'

And Maximilian—would it put him in a good mood too, to have that beautiful woman being charming to him? Now why had that thought even occurred to her...?

She slowly joined the young girl. 'And maybe if it sweetens her up enough you won't have to apologise,' she said.

'Oh, I'll still have to apologise. Abjectly.' Jennie rolled her eyes expressively. 'But an hour alone with Daddy could mean the difference between Celia's accepting it gracefully or being a real pain in the—about it!' she amended with feeling.

She couldn't help returning the young girl's cheeky grin, finding her almost endearing at that moment, shaking her head ruefully as she followed Jennie down the back stairs to the kitchen. 'You really have it all worked out, don't you?' she said admiringly.

Jennie smiled up at her. 'It's called surviving in an adult world.' She made a face.

'Maybe,' Sophie accepted ruefully, knowing she had probably used similar subterfuge herself to get a lighter punishment as a child when she had offended her parents with her behaviour. 'And I'm sorry to disappoint you,' she added teasingly, 'but I'm afraid at the moment your father isn't alone; he has Paul with him.'

Jennie gave another glance back at her as they neared the kitchen. 'Who's Paul?' She looked puzzled.

'I would have thought you knew him,' she said in some surprise. 'He's——'

'Ssh!' Jennie instructed impatiently as she came to an abrupt halt at the kitchen door. 'Daddy is in there telling *your* aunt that *my* aunt will be joining us for this late lunch we're all eventually supposed to be having! I know it's my fault that we're late,' she acknowledged at Sophie's pointed look. 'But I'm starving. Oh, God, I hope Daddy didn't see me just then!' She pressed back against the wall so that they couldn't be seen through the glass-topped door that led into the kitchen from this back stair.

No angry Maximilian came bursting out of the kitchen, so Sophie could only assume that he hadn't spotted Jennie—and consequently her also—skulking out here!

But she had forgotten all about lunch herself since waking up so late in the day, and, as Jennie had just pointed out, it was way past lunchtime now. A late lunch; it was going to be more like afternoon tea! And it seemed she was going to meet Celia at the meal too, something she wasn't exactly looking forward to, she had to admit— a feeling she had in common with Jennie. But for different reasons. Just that brief glimpse of Celia had been enough to make her aware of the sharp contrast between the two of them, Sophie short and tomboyish, with freckles and unruly red hair, her clothing casual in the extreme. The other woman, probably aged somewhere in her late twenties, was sure to treat her on the same patronising level as she no doubt did Jennie. Just what her self-esteem needed!

'Come on,' Jennie encouraged impatiently, the coast obviously having become clear while Sophie indulged in the tortuous self-doubt just looking at the lovely Celia had induced. 'Mm, as lovely as usual, Mrs Craine,' she said appreciatively after picking up one of the cakes that had been left out on a rack to cool and biting into it, her mouth now full of the light sponge.

'Miss Jennifer!' Aunt Millie had turned from the cooker now, the young girl who came in at the weekends to help out also turning to look at them. 'Sophie!' Her aunt's eyes widened condemningly as she saw she had followed Jennie into the room.

'Can't stop, Aunt Millie,' she called out as she hurried after Jennie, the young girl only having paused long enough to pick up another cake before going outside into the sunshine. Sophie hadn't dared to grab a cake for herself, even though the sight and smell of them had been enough to make her mouth water. Jennie had a double advantage over her now; Sophie hadn't had any lunch *or* breakfast!

Jennie saw her empty hands. 'Aren't you hungry? Of course you are,' she answered her own question as she saw Sophie's expression. 'Then why didn't you——? Ah...the dreaded "aunt" syndrome,' she said knowingly. 'Here.' She thrust the second cake at Sophie, munching hungrily on her own cake as she made her way determinedly towards the stables.

Sophie was sure, that if Maximilian came to hear of the incident, he would have expected her to refuse to eat the stolen cake, that to eat it would be to condone Jennie's outrageous behaviour. But at that moment Sophie didn't care what Maximilian would think; the rumbling of her stomach told her it would be sheer stupidity not to eat the cake!

But as she hurriedly followed Jennie across the stable-yard she did reflect on exactly *who* was supposed to be in charge of *whom*; Jennie certainly had a mind of her own, and a will to go with it, and, with Sophie's more easygoing nature of live-and-let-live, that could prove to be a problem over the next few days.

Jennie already had one of the stable doors open, throwing a saddle up on to the back of a beautiful black mare, barely glancing up from the task of tightening the girth as Sophie came to stand in the doorway. 'Until I can see just how well you ride, you'd better take Becky,' she advised lightly. 'She's docile and obedient, and she's in the next stall to this one,' she added dismissively.

If Maximilian and his daughter struck sparks off each other when they were together, it was easy to see why, Sophie muttered to herself as she moved to the stall next door! They were both so incredibly—— Good God, Jennie believed *this* horse was 'docile and obedient',

Sophie groaned inwardly as she opened the door to the neighbouring stall and found herself eyeball to eyeball with a very feisty-looking young chestnut mare. She was undoubtedly a beautiful horse, but 'docile and obedient' seemed a little hard to believe!

Not that Sophie considered herself a bad rider; in fact she had ridden here on the estate a lot as a child. But it was a couple of years now since she had been up on the back of a horse, and she could already feel the strain to all those unused muscles if she had to master this horse today.

'Hurry up, Sophie, we haven't got—good grief!' Jennie had obviously finished saddling her own horse, and had decided to come and chivvy Sophie along. But she looked as puzzled by the horse in this second stall as Sophie was apprehensive. 'What on earth...?' She dropped the leader reins to her own horse now, moving slowly forward to get a closer look at this chestnut mare, murmuring softly to the horse as she approached it. 'What are you doing here, Lady?' she crooned. 'You're a little far away from—Jenkins, what's Lady doing here?' she frowned at the stable-hand who seemed to have appeared from nowhere behind them.

All that Sophie cared about at that moment was that this *wasn't* Becky, her relief enormous at the realisation that she didn't have to ride this particular horse at all. The mare shied away from Jennie now, snorting warningly as she did so.

'If you intend going riding, Jennifer, then I suggest you do so without delay,' rasped the all too familiar voice of Maximillian Grant, his expression grim as he approached from the house. 'And leave Jenkins to get on with his work.'

Indignant colour darkened Jennie's cheeks at this unwarranted reprimand from her father; she hadn't been stopping Jenkins from working! 'I was only——'

'I'm well aware of what you "were only",' Maximilian bit out harshly, giving a brief nod to his middle-aged employee. Jenkins instantly refastened the door to Lady's stall. 'Haven't you already caused enough disruption for one day?' Maximilian turned on his daughter once again as she and Sophie stood watching the procedure.

'It seems I do that by merely existing!' Jennie spat the words out defiantly before swinging herself up on to the back of the black mare, tossing her head back rebelliously before lightly digging her heels in to urge her mount out of the confining yard, the sound of thundering hoofs quickly following.

'Well?' Maximilian looked at Sophie glacially as she stood helplessly by watching all of this. 'I thought you'd decided you wanted the job?'

This really was the rudest, most arrogant family she had ever had the misfortune to meet!

'Which horse do you want me to ride?' she prompted exasperatedly; she could hardly go after Jennie without a horse.

'Jenkins will saddle Becky for you. Quickly,' he ordered the other man grimly. 'Lunch will be served in exactly forty minutes,' he said, turning dismissively back to Sophie.

And they had better not be so much as a second later than that, Sophie guessed from his tone, or else she and Jennie would be in for another tongue-lashing from this man. Lunch promised to be a very jolly affair!

It was exactly forty minutes later when she and Jennie went downstairs to the main sitting-room to join Maximilian and Celia before lunch; Sophie knew it was exactly forty minutes because Jennie had insisted on delaying until the last possible moment once she was aware of the request, deliberately lingering over her shower and then getting dressed. Request? Hah! Jennie hadn't been fooled for a moment by being told it was that, had known even better than Sophie that it was a dictate; Maximilian had never *requested* anything in his life, had probably been demanding in his cradle, and saw no reason to change!

But, as Sophie had guessed it might be, a young female version of him was just as difficult to deal with, and the more she tried to hurry Jennie along so that they shouldn't be late and earn yet another black mark, the more determined Jennie seemed to be to dither, spending what seemed like hours choosing for her wardrobe what to wear, and then wandering off into the bathroom with them as if she had all day to shower and dress. Sophie had left her to it. She didn't know which was the most infuriating out of father and daughter—which the more stubborn, the mountain or Mahammet—but she did know that neither of them was willing to give an inch, and that it could be very wearing for the people who came into contact with them, specifically her!

As it was it had taken her almost ten minutes of the specified time even to locate Jennie, having ridden Becky—who *was*, thankfully, docile and obedient— haphazardly over the grounds looking for her, finally coming upon her quite by chance near the stream that ran half a mile away from the main house, the black mare, which had obviously been ridden hard, taking a much needed drink.

Pale blue eyes glared at Sophie warningly as she approached, silencing any questions she might have cared to ask, and although the two of them had ridden along together after that, Sophie had continued to respect the young girl's privacy. No doubt when Jennie was ready to talk she would do so; a lack of articulation didn't seem to be a problem with her!

Her own denims and T-shirt had had a definite smell of horses about them once she had undressed in preparation for her own shower, but she was very limited in the things she had brought with her, having packed in the first place with the idea of being companion to a teenage girl, not with any intention of taking part in a fashion show!

But even that brief glimpse of Celia's dress she had had earlier had been enough to tell her it was a designer label, and, also considering the immaculate way Maximilian always dressed, she didn't think he would welcome her going down for the meal wearing her spare pair of denims. But her wardrobe *was* limited, and she wasn't altogether sure he was going to find the tight black leggings and over-long thin woollen jumper in a shade of green that made her eyes appear the same dark colour any more acceptable.

Jennie had still been in the bathroom when Sophie went up to check on her, and so Sophie had gone back to her own room to collect her horse-smelling clothing to take through to the utility room, and throwing them into the washing-machine before going in search of Jennie once again; one more minute, and their forty minutes would be up!

Thankfully, Jennie was just coming down the stairs when Sophie went out into the hallway, although the young girl's eyes widened as she joined her. 'Aunt Celia is going to hate you!' she said gleefully.

God, that was just what she needed to hear! 'Why?' she groaned incredulously.

Jennie grinned in anticipation. 'Because you have great legs, and you're young enough to get away with wearing those leggings,' she explained with satisfaction.

From what Sophie had seen of the other woman's legs, there was certainly nothing wrong with them.

'You also look sexy as hell in them,' Jennie added with relish for what she was sure was going to be a momentous meeting between her aunt and Sophie, and it was obvious that Jennie didn't mean her anticipation in a bitchy way—at least, not as far as Sophie was concerned, anyway!

'Jennie!' she reproved distractedly, inwardly wondering if she had time to go and change again—all the time knowing that she didn't.

'But you do,' Jennie was deliberately obtuse. 'Are you sure you aren't Daddy's latest mistress?' She quirked mocking brows.

'Very funny!' Sophie sighed her impatience. 'Come on, let's go in and face them—before we get into trouble for being *late* this time!'

Consequently, even though the two of them arrived exactly on time for the late meal, because of the conversation they had just had in the hallway about Sophie's clothes she felt at a distinct disadvantage, self-conscious in the revealing leggings, something she had never felt when she'd worn them before.

Maximilian and Celia were alone in the sitting-room, Paul Wiseman conspicuously absent—because he had felt like an unwanted third?—the couple both turning towards the doorway as Sophie and Jennie entered.

Sophie looked at Maximilian with a certain amount of trepidation, noting the way his gaze narrowed on Jennie, but seemed satisfied with the tailored black trousers she wore with a loose silky blouse in the same ice-blue colour as her eyes. His gaze didn't pass as quickly over Sophie, though, and she could feel herself starting to squirm uncomfortably as he slowly took in her appearance. She turned away quickly, only to find herself looking straight into violet-coloured eyes that were looking her up and down with the hostility Jennie had predicted!

Celia stood up, gracefully crossing the room to kiss Jennie briefly on the cheek before turning to look at Sophie. 'Your father didn't tell me you were bringing a school-friend home with you, Jennifer,' she drawled with a challenging lift to one black winged brow.

Ouch! Jennie was right: her aunt *had* taken an instant dislike to her. She knew her lack of height, and the freckles, detracted from her age, but there was no way, despite that, that she looked like a school-friend of Jennie's! She certainly wouldn't have minded looking the way Jennie did, but there was no way she could be mistaken for a sixteen-year-old.

Maximilian stood up in one smooth movement. 'This is the young lady I told you about, Celia,' he drawled drily. 'She's here to help keep Jennie amused.'

The sweepingly disparaging look Celia gave Sophie told her the other woman thought she was *more* than capable of amusing a teenager! Maximilian could have chosen his words a little more—carefully. Or perhaps he had, she realised slowly, as she saw the glitter of laughter in the depths of his eyes.

'Celia Taylor—Sophie Gordon,' he introduced mockingly.

'Mrs Taylor.' Sophie held out her hand politely. Even if she did sense that the other woman already disliked her, she wasn't going to give Maximilian any reason, if she could help it, to criticise her own manner towards Celia Taylor.

What a strange family they were, she thought, not for the first time. A father and daughter who were so arrogantly alike that they didn't even realise it, and couldn't hope to understand each other because of that blindness. And now the sister of Maximilian's dead wife and Jennie's mother, who thought she had some sort of proprietorial claim on both of them, and warned off all other females because of it. Even Sophie, it seemed. Which was ridiculous. Or was it...? Her cheeks warmed as she remembered being close to Maximilian last night.

They warmed even more as she realised that that was how she thought of him now—simply as Maximilian...

'*Ms* Taylor,' the other woman corrected her sharply, eyes narrowed on Sophie's flushed cheeks.

'Celia is a career-woman, Sophie,' Maximilian supplied with an affectionate smile for his sister-in-law. 'She's never married, never felt the need to have one male permanently in her life,' he added teasingly.

'That isn't quite true, Max.' Celia moved languidly to his side, putting her arm through the crook of his as she smiled up at him invitingly. 'The right man just hasn't asked me yet,' she corrected huskily.

Jennie gave Sophie an 'I told you so' raise of her eyebrows, and Sophie quickly averted her gaze so that her charge shouldn't think she was sharing the conspiratorial behaviour with her. Nor should 'Max', Sophie inwardly pleaded as she saw that he hadn't missed the exchange, and was even now looking at her with narrowed eyes that contained not a little anger—and a lot of displeasure!

She turned away from him just as quickly, frantically searching in her mind for something to say that would divert his attention away from that look Jennie had tried to exchange with her. 'What work do you do, Ms Taylor?' she said with forced brightness; she was going to be a nervous wreck at the end of this week if she had to keep skating on ice in this way!

Violet eyes looked Sophie up and down before the other woman answered her in a somewhat bored voice, 'I'm a fashion editor,' and the magazine she mentioned after that had been heard of by everyone.

Sophie might have guessed! Everything about this woman, from the top of her glossy black head to her daintily clad feet, spoke of stylish elegance. 'That's nice,' Sophie returned lamely, not knowing what else she could say to such a statement. She, who wasn't usually *ever* at a loss for words!

'I happen to think so.' The other woman nodded dismissively. 'I'd be pleased to give you a few tips some time, if you're ever interested.'

Ooh, ouch again! Strange, she had never before made an enemy of someone without even having had to say a word! As far as she was aware, she didn't go around making enemies anyway, though it seemed that all that was required of her this time was that she be female and in the same house as Maximilian Grant.

Seeing the two of them together like this, Maximilian and Celia's easy familiarity with each other, Sophie was no nearer knowing if Maximilian had 'the hots' for his sister-in-law. What she had learnt, however, was that, even if he was attracted to Celia in return, the other woman was far from sure of him, and obviously saw all other women as rivals for his affection.

'Thank you,' Sophie returned non-committally. 'I think my aunt may be ready for us to go into lunch now,' she added with some relief as she saw Aunt Millie signalling to her from the doorway.

'Which we are *all* more than ready for,' Maximilian said knowingly as he extricated himself from Celia Taylor's clinging arm. 'Thank you, Mrs Craine.' He smiled warmly at his housekeeper. 'I'm sorry you've been put to all this trouble.'

'We've all been put to a lot of trouble today on behalf of one young lady.' Celia gave Jennie a pointed look, her brows raised reprovingly.

So Jennie wasn't going to get away with this so lightly after all, Sophie realised sympathetically as the young girl flushed self-consciously at the same time as she gave her aunt a resentful glare for bringing up the subject. That scowl certainly wasn't going to help her cause, if the gathering thunderclouds of anger on Maximilian's brow were anything to go by!

'I believe you owe your aunt an apology, Jennifer,' he rasped in that autocratic voice that was warning enough. 'I'm sure Celia had better things to do this afternoon than drive over here because you had disappeared,' he added with stern disapproval.

'She didn't *have* to drive over here at all,' Jennie snapped rebelliously. 'Although goodness knows, she only lives ten miles away; it's not as if she had to drive to the other side of the country!'

'Jennifer!' Maximilian still didn't raise his voice, but the warning it contained had risen audibly.

A warning Jennie was in no mood to heed. 'Well, it's not,' she defended stubbornly. 'And I could have telephoned her later and——'

'Her *name* is "Aunt Celia",' Maximilian cut in icily, his body rigid with anger. 'I believed allowing you to go for a ride before lunch would cool your temper somewhat,' he continued coldly. 'But if anything you appear to be even ruder than you were before. Perhaps going up to your bedroom and not having any lunch might just——'

'That's not fair!' Jennie protested heatedly, her eyes blazing with fury.

Maximilian's mouth twisted. 'A lot of life is unfair, Jennifer,' he began derisively.

'Oh, spare me *that* lecture. This is *my* life we're talking about, not yours, not Aunt Celia's.' Her voice rose frustratedly. 'I'm the one being punished just because I didn't want to go to Aunt Celia's for the holidays——'

'Not *just* because of that,' her father corrected harshly.

'Oh, no, of course not,' Jennie choked, past any sort of reason now, her face flushed with anger. 'I'm being punished because I'm here at all, aren't I!' She glared at her father. 'Life has been "unfair" to *you* because you have such a nuisance for a daughter! Because we both know that if Mummy had still been alive I wouldn't have been here at all; neither of us would——'

'Jennifer!' This time Maximilian's voice brooked no argument. Absolutely none. From anyone.

Looking at the two of them, so much alike, both so angry, Jennie's eyes full of unshed tears now, a nerve pulsating in Maximilian's rigidly clenched jaw, his eyes like chips of blue ice, Sophie felt so sorry for both of them, and wished there were something she could do or say that would alleviate the strain from the situation. But she knew so little about either of them yet, had no idea of the deep emotions behind Jennie's obviously heartfelt accusations.

And the little she did know put Maximilian in a very bad light as far as she was concerned. If Celia Taylor only lived ten miles away, and Maximilian was staying at this house anyway, then why on earth *had* he intended sending her to stay with her aunt for the week, especially when the original plan had been for Jennie to stay here? Had Maximilian changed the plan *because* he was staying here and now didn't want Jennifer to as well? And what did Jennie's comment about her mother mean? It was all a little too complex at the moment for her to know quite how to deal with things for the best.

But, despite being at a distinct disadvantage where the relationship between father and daughter was concerned, Sophie felt she ought to at least try to say something to defuse the situation a little—especially as Celia Taylor didn't seem about to do anything to help out in that direction, and was watching Jennie with narrowed eyes.

Sophie gave a bright smile. 'Maybe if we all have some lunch and talk afterwards——'

'Didn't you hear my father, Sophie?' Jennie scorned, still glaring at him. 'Like a child, I've been ordered to my room——'

'Maybe when you stop acting like one, and can show me you're a responsible adult, I won't treat you like a child,' Maximilian said with icy dismissal, obviously not budging by so much as an inch over his decision that Jennie should go to her bedroom.

Sophie watched in dismay as Jennie turned on her heel and stormed out of the room, the door slamming shut behind her. Couldn't Maximilian see that Jennie behaved in exactly this way because it seemed to her to be the only way she could get his attention, albeit in an angry way? Until he *did* see that, Jennie's behaviour wasn't likely to improve.

Sophie looked at Maximilian now with pained eyes. 'Perhaps I should go after her and——'

'No!' he rasped coldly, challenge etched into the harshness of his face. 'As far as I'm aware, you haven't eaten since last night. And Jennifer will be better for being given time to think about her actions rather than tumbling headlong into one disastrous situation after another,' he announced firmly.

'I couldn't agree with you more, darling Max,' Celia Taylor once again linked her arm with his, gazing up at him warmly. 'Josephine obviously spoilt the child, and you've been left to sort the problem out,' she sighed sympathetically.

If this was the way Maximilian intended 'sorting the problem out', then he wasn't going to be very successful, Sophie was afraid! What Jennie appeared to need was her father's time and attention, if not exactly his approval, rather than this constant clash of wills the two of them seemed to have.

And that didn't seem about to be forthcoming. Instead, with Jennie's departure, Sophie now seemed to have been left to have lunch alone with Celia Taylor and Maximilian. It was enough to deprive her of *her* appetite!

CHAPTER SIX

'YOU can take that "I could have told you" grin off your face!' Sophie scowled across the bedroom at Jennie. 'Or I'll take those sandwiches back!'

'No way!' Jennie put a protective hand over the plate of sandwiches she was munching her way through, sitting cross-legged on top of the lace duvet on her bed. 'I'm absolutely starving!' she groaned.

'You deserve to be!' Sophie said with feeling, finding it difficult still to forgive the young girl for leaving her to such a fate.

Lunch, for Sophie, had been every bit as awful as she had thought it might be. And it had nothing to do with the food, Aunt Millie's cooking every bit as good as it had always been; it had been the company that had grated. Well...*Celia Taylor* had grated. Well...actually, it had been the way the other woman constantly felt the need to touch and flirt with Maximilian that had *grated*, if Sophie was completely honest with herself.

She had been jealous of the other woman's familiarity with him!

Not that Maximilian had even seemed to notice the way Celia was always touching his hand or arm as she talked to him, his attention not having been completely on the conversation. Although he answered Celia politely enough, his thoughts seemed to be elsewhere. With Jennie, Sophie hoped, and how he was going to set about bridging that gulf that seemed to be ever widening between himself and his daughter. Because, if he didn't stop it now, in a couple of years' time it was going to be too late, the breach irreversible.

But even though Sophie had refused dessert and coffee, the meal had gone on far too long for her comfort. The other woman had greeted this refusal with a lightly mocking comment about her 'having to watch her figure'—something Celia herself didn't seem to bother about as she accepted a huge piece of the home-made lemon meringue pie. *Sophie* hadn't refused be-cause she wouldn't have liked a piece of the pie herself, or indeed because she had to watch the calories; she had never been prone to fat. No, she had refused purely and simply because she wanted to get away from the nauseating display the other woman was making of herself with Maximilian!

Maximilian had tersely granted her request to be ex-cused, and Sophie had hurried from the dining-room before he could think of a reason to change his mind, going straight to the kitchen to make some sandwiches for Jennie and grab a can of Coke for each of them— this much to the disapproval of her aunt.

But Sophie just couldn't bear the thought of Jennie having to go hungry, especially when she was convinced it had been Celia Taylor's baiting of her that had ac-tually caused Jennie to lose her temper in the way she had; the raven-haired beauty was enough to make Sophie grind her teeth after only an hour's acquaintance, so goodness knew how Jennie felt about the woman after being forced into her company all of her life!

She had carried the tray of sandwiches and drinks up the back stairs, carefully avoiding being seen by either Maximilian or Celia Taylor.

Jennie had been lying on her back on the bed, although she had visibly brightened at the sight of the sandwiches and drink.

'Aunt Celia worked her usual magic charm, did she?' Jennie said knowingly, biting into another sandwich. 'Can you blame me, now that you've met her,' she grimaced, 'for not wanting to spend my holiday at her house?'

Sophie was still puzzled at the need for Jennie to do so when the other woman lived so close anyway. But at the moment she thought it best not to bring that subject up with Jennie; it might be best if Jennie avoided being bad-tempered and resentful for a while. And no doubt Maximilian had his reasons for arranging things this way.

Although at this precise moment in time Sophie couldn't for the life of her think of one that would be even remotely acceptable!

At the same time, she knew she couldn't encourage Jennie's disrespectful behaviour towards her aunt. 'She could teach you a lot about fashion,' she suggested— because, for the moment, with the memory of the other woman's acidic company still so vivid, Sophie couldn't actually think of anything more favourable to say about her!

Jennie gave her a pitying look, not fooled for a moment. 'Is that the best you can do?'

As it happened, yes! How could she sit and spout platitudes about a woman who had made no secret of the fact that she didn't particularly like her—*or* the way she dressed? A woman, moreover, who had made it obvious, from her almost total exclusion of Sophie from the conversation, that she didn't particularly like sitting down to lunch with one of the 'hired help' anyway!

'I don't think we should——' She broke off guiltily as a knock sounded on the bedroom door. Jennie quickly hid the half-eaten sandwiches and cans of Coke under the bed, choking down her mouthful of food, giving Sophie a pained grimace before going to open the door.

To the immense relief of both of them it was only Aunt Millie who stood outside. Only? From the thunderous expression on her aunt's face, this wasn't a social call!

'You, young lady, will get us all shot if your father finds out we've brought you food up here when he told you you couldn't have any lunch today!' She frowned disapprovingly at Jennie as the young girl took the sandwiches and drinks from beneath her bed and resumed eating.

'You didn't bring it, remember, Aunt Millie, *I* did,' Sophie soothed, still puzzled by her aunt's expression. It couldn't be the food and drink that was still upsetting her; she had already had her say on that downstairs earlier. What had happened now? Sophie wondered wearily.

'As for you, Sophie——' her aunt turned on her sharply now, as if sensing her resignation '—what have you been up to now?'

She frowned. She had been hoping her aunt would be able to tell *her* that. 'Apart from the sandwiches and drink for Jennie...?'

'One presumes so, yes!' Aunt Millie snapped, deeply agitated. 'I'm sure Mr Grant would have said something to me first if *that* were it...' she murmured thoughtfully.

'Then as far as I know,' Sophie shrugged, 'nothing.'

Her aunt's mouth firmed. 'Well, Mr Grant has asked to see you in his study immediately, so you must have done something!'

The study again, she realised heavily. But as far as she was aware she hadn't committed any other misdemeanour he could haul her over the coals about, not in the short space since the last time, anyway! It certainly couldn't have been anything she said during lunch; she had hardly spoken, and her manners had been impeccable—even when she had been sorely provoked by some of Celia Taylor's more cutting remarks towards her.

'Maybe not, Aunt Millie.' She stood up slowly, trying to look on the bright side. 'Perhaps Mr Grant is just anxious to discuss some of the arrangements for the next week with me.' Goodness knew, there had been little enough time for that earlier.

Her aunt relaxed slightly, although her frown remained. 'Do you think that could be it?' she said uncertainly.

Sophie certainly hoped so! Although she was actually far from sure... 'That will be it, Aunt Millie,' she dismissed confidently.

'Well... Immediately, then, Sophie,' her aunt reminded before leaving, although a perplexed frown still furrowed her brow.

Jennie didn't look so easily convinced. '*Do* you think that's it?' she frowned darkly.

Sophie grimaced. 'I'm hoping so.' Although she didn't, in actual fact, hold out much hope of being right; what had she done now?

'I'm coming with you.' Jennie stood up decisively, her sandwich and drink put aside. 'If Aunt Celia has—no,' she frowned anew as she looked down on to the driveway. 'She seems to have gone, and if she had been making mischief she would have stayed around long enough to watch what happened.' Jennie grimaced.

She certainly seemed to have got the measure of her aunt, no matter what Maximilian might think of her maturity! 'I don't think your coming down with me would be a good idea,' Sophie refused ruefully. 'Although I do appreciate the offer.'

'But——'

'If I need the cavalry, I'll call, hmm?' she prompted self-derisively, grinning with much more confidence than she actually felt.

But her smile faded as soon as she was out in the hallway. And when she arrived at Maximilian's study to find Paul Wiseman was in there with him, albeit standing unobtrusively across the room near the window, Sophie knew she had been right to feel apprehensive; Maximilian already had *his* cavalry in the room with him—although it was doubtful he ever felt in need of it! Just what was going on here?

Maximilian's expression was grim as he looked across at her still standing in the doorway. 'Come in and close the door, Miss Gordon,' he instructed coolly. 'Although it isn't Miss anything, is it, but *Mrs* Ames?' he added softly from behind her as she did as instructed.

Sophie spun around, her face paling, freckles standing out lividly against the white, her eyes wide green pools of distress at this unexpected attack.

Maximilian continued to look at her grimly, seemingly unmoved by the obvious shock he had just given her. 'Leave us, Paul,' he rasped harshly to the other man, the coldness of his gaze never leaving Sophie's stricken face.

The other man stepped forward from the shadows. 'I don't think that would be advisable in the circumstances, Mr Grant——' He broke off abruptly as that cold blue gaze flashed warningly in his direction, a ruddy hue darkening his cheeks as Maximilian continued to look at him. 'I'll go and check in with Jenkins,' he finally nodded agreement before striding quickly from the room, the door closing quietly but forcefully behind him.

Sophie hadn't really been listening to the exchange between the two men, her mind racing frantically as she wondered how on earth Maximilian had found out *that* particular piece of information about her. She hadn't been officially Mrs anything for almost two years now, and she hadn't used the name Ames for a lot longer than that.

The mistake she had so wilfully made at only eighteen. A mistake that had haunted her long after it should have been over. And it looked as if it was about to haunt her once again!

'Sit down.' Maximilian spoke slightly more gently this time. 'Before you fall down,' he added impatiently when she made no attempt to move.

Sophie sat, too numbed to do anything else. It wasn't that she had ever deceived anyone about the existence of her marriage; she had just never broadcast the fact either. But Maximilian obviously didn't like the fact that he hadn't been informed.

Cavalry—she had a feeling she was going to need a *miracle* to get her out of this!

'Well?' he said finally, as some of the colour returned to her cheeks.

What did he want her to say? ''I—I reverted back to my maiden name after my husband—died,' she told him woodenly.

'There was a bit more to it than that, Sophie.' Maximilian said tersely, glancing down at a paper on the desktop in front of him. 'It says here——'

'What *is* that?' she demanded incredulously, leaning forward to snatch the sheet of paper up in her hands, quickly reading what was typed there, looking up at him with darkly accusing eyes once she had done so. Maximilian hadn't moved, hadn't attempted to stop her, and was looking at her now with cold eyes. 'You had no right,' she choked. 'No right at all!' It was all there, in black and white, all the details of her life starkly laid out. 'Where did you get this?' Her hand tightly clenched the piece of paper, crumpling one side of it.

Maximilian shrugged dismissively. 'Paul——'

'Your so-called assistant; I should have guessed!' she dismissed scornfully. 'No wonder he didn't join us for lunch,' she scoffed. 'He was too busy putting all this together!' She threw the sheet of paper back on Maximilian's desk. 'You should give him a pay-rise, Mr Grant; he's obviously very good at his job!'

'Sophie, will you just calm down?' Maximilian snapped impatiently. 'If you do, we may just be able to sort this situation out——'

'What is there to sort out?' She glared at him resentfully. 'You obviously had me checked out because you're very careful whom you allow near your family.' She shook her head. 'I'm obviously totally unsuitable——'

'I didn't say that,' he cut in irritably, obviously not accustomed to having situations taken out of his control in this way.

But Sophie didn't particularly care how he felt at that moment, was too raw herself to be concerned with his feelings. 'You didn't have to.' She stood up abruptly. 'Don't worry, Mr Grant, I'll save you the unpleasant task of sacking me and just leave quietly. All I ask is that you don't blame Aunt Millie for any of this; like the rest of my family, she was against my marriage from the start,' Sophie recalled dully; it was far too late to wish she had listened to any of them. With the usual rebelliousness of youth, she had thought she knew better. She had learnt, the hard way, that sometimes people who were older had a wider knowledge of people too, and that it sometimes helped to listen to them.

Maximilian's mouth tightened. 'I have no intention of "blaming" your aunt for anything,' he denied with impatience. 'Just as——'

'Thank you.' Sophie nodded her satisfaction with this much of a concession at least. 'I'll tell Jennie that I've had a change of plan, if you like; I don't want to be the cause of any friction between the two of you.' She and Jennie had only known each other a short time, but she was sure the young girl liked *her* as much as she was coming to like her.

Maximilian straightened. 'I can handle my own daughter, thank you,' he rasped dismissively.

For all that he might be quite capable in most other things, from the little she had witnessed between him and Jennie, when it came to his daughter he was at a complete loss! 'I'll clear things with her anyway,' Sophie shrugged. 'Now I have to go and pack, and——'

'*I did not say I wanted you to leave!*' Maximilian burst out exasperatedly, standing up impatiently, blond hair falling endearingly across his forehead as he did so, his hands clenched into fists at his sides.

'I saved you the bother,' she accepted ruefully. 'But, despite what you say, I would just like to give you one word of advice,' she added with intensity, not willing to just walk away from this situation without at least trying to salvage something from it, if not for herself, then for Jennie.

He became very still, eyes narrowed. 'Advice?' he repeated in a dangerously soft voice.

'Hmm,' she nodded with a grimace. 'If you carry on treating Jennie—she doesn't like the name Jennifer, by the way——' she put in with a grimace '—if you carry on treating her as a child, then she will continue to act like one. A spoilt madam of a child, as only a rebellious sixteen-year-old can be. I was married at eighteen, remember,' she added pointedly.

He frowned darkly. 'Are you saying Jennif—my daughter could do something like that too?' he demanded harshly.

'I wouldn't know,' she shrugged. 'I don't know if Jennie has anyone in her life at the moment. What I *do* know is that she has a definite mind of her own, and it wouldn't do to underestimate it. Just try thinking of yourself at the same age,' Sophie added ruefully, sure he had been a determined child as much as he was now an arrogant man.

He was scowling now. 'You have known my daughter for exactly...' he looked down at the plain gold watch on his wrist '...Three hours,' he told her with hard derision. 'I think after sixteen years I know her slightly better than you do.' He ignored the remark she had made about Jennie being like him.

The look Sophie gave him was sad. 'Do you?' she said quietly, shrugging with resignation. 'Then there's nothing else I can say.' She had tried, she couldn't do any more.

'Sophie!' he called out impatiently as she turned to leave.

'I'm sorry,' she choked, the tears that had been threatening for some time, blinding her now. 'I—have to go!'

'For God's sake——'

'Please!' She was desperate to get away from him now, before she broke down completely, pulling away from the hold he now had of her arm.

'Sophie, for God's sake listen! If you won't listen——!' he grated frustratedly, pulling her even closer.

She couldn't see, was completely blinded by the tears now, only aware of the hard savagery of his lips against hers, the anger in his body as he held her moulded against his hardness, his mouth plundering hers now, demanding a response from her, a response she dared not give, pulling away from him to run from the room before she became just a burbling wreck.

She wasn't usually this emotional, had learnt not to be, couldn't afford to be. She knew that it was the mention of that early marriage she so regretted that had broken down her defences. Married at eighteen, separated not six months later, and a widow at twenty before her divorce could even be applied for. She was sorry Malcolm had died, of course she was, didn't like the waste of any human life, but she was even sorrier, if he had to die at all, that it had happened when it did.

Because officially she had still been Mrs Malcolm Ames. And Malcolm's debts had become *her* debts . . .

She had been working on her Open University course for almost a year when Malcolm died, and his death had come as a double blow to her: the shock of his dying at all, and because it seemed that, now she finally had her life sorted out into some sort of direction, it might be destroyed all over again. It had only been because of sheer hard work and—yes, sacrifice, on her part, that she had managed to work to pay off some of those debts at the same time as carrying on with her Open University course.

For almost two years now she had held her life together almost day to day, getting jobs when she could—like this one—and really having to struggle when she couldn't work. And then, suddenly, from out of the blue, that adolescent mistake—and marrying Malcolm had certainly been that!—would come back to haunt her once again, and just when she least expected it. Like now, when she had thought the past well and truly behind her.

How dared Maximilian have her investigated in that way? Just who did he think he and his family were, that he needed to pry into other people's lives? Well, whoever it was, Sophie wanted no part of it. In the past people had always been quite happy to judge her on her own merits, not those of her or her dead husband's past, and if Maximilian Grant couldn't do that, it was his loss not——

'What's wrong?'

She hadn't noticed Jennie waiting out in the hallway, so deep in thought had she been. But as the young girl clasped hold of her upper arm Sophie had no choice but to at least acknowledge her.

Jennie looked at her searchingly—and she obviously didn't like what she saw! 'Sophie, tell me what's wrong?'

The resemblance between father and daughter was too great at the moment, both of them arrogant in the extreme as far as Sophie was concerned. She wrenched her arm away to glare up at the young girl; even the fact that she was forced to do that, because of Jennie's superior height, annoyed her at that moment.

'Ask your father, Jennie,' she snapped, completely forgetting in that moment of anger that she had said she would clear it with Jennie herself about her leaving. 'Or Paul,' she added bitterly. 'He seems to be the one with all the answers!'

Jennie shook her head, a puzzled frown between her eyes. 'That's the second time you've mentioned someone called Paul, but I don't know anyone of that name.' She shrugged. 'Are you sure you——?'

'Look, I don't care *what* his name is.' Sophie was starting to feel slightly hysterical now. 'Please just go and talk to your father, Jennie, if you want to know anything else,' she choked. 'I have to go and pack.'

'Pack...?' Jennie looked dumbfounded by this statement. 'But—I'll go and talk to my father.' She nodded grimly at Sophie's pained expression.

'I wish you would,' Sophie nodded, turning to go through to the back of the house where the servants' quarters were, carefully avoiding the kitchen, where she knew her aunt and May, the girl who came in from the village at weekends to help out, would be busy preparing dinner. It was going to be difficult enough explaining this 'she was going—no, she was staying—no, she was going again' situation to her aunt as it was; she certainly didn't feel up to doing it just now.

She sat down heavily on the bed once she reached the sanctuary of the bedroom she had been given, needing just to sit and catch her breath before she set about putting her things into her hold-all.

She felt raw, exposed, the disaster of her marriage laid open to the whole household. Because Maximilian, when asked, would no doubt tell Jennie exactly why she was so unsuitable, explain that Sophie's husband had been a gambler, that when he died he had smashed up the only asset he had left: a flashy sports car. What people didn't realise, including Sophie herself when she had first met Malcolm, was that the car was an old one, a fact that was obscured by the personalised number-plate and the mint condition he liked to keep it in.

Oh, Malcolm apparently had all the trappings of wealth, always did everything in an extravagantly expensive style. Their own wedding had been an example of that; all of Malcolm's so-called friends invited to the reception that had been thrown at one of the most prestigious hotels in London. And for the weeks and months that followed the wedding Sophie had struggled single-handed to pay off the bills that flooded in! Malcolm's answer, whenever she brought up the subject of the bills with him, was that when he had a big win at the casino he would pay them all off in one grand gesture. The casino had come as yet another surprise to Sophie; Malcolm seemed to go there five nights out of seven, had apparently always done so, even during the time they were going out together, more often than not going on there after leaving her at the end of an evening out together.

Only there had been no 'big wins' during their brief marriage, and as the weeks passed Malcolm became more and more morose and agitated, finally restoring to blaming this run of bad luck on his marriage. And Sophie.

The weeks that followed this accusation had been worse than the worrying ones before—because now Malcolm had something to focus his frustration on. And he lost no opportunity to do so, growing even angrier when she ceased trying to placate him and just wearily accepted the verbal diatribe, until finally this verbal anger turned to a physical one.

Sophie had withstood weeks of verbal abuse, but physical violence was something she couldn't stand, and she knew it was time to leave. The love she had been so sure she felt towards Malcolm at the start of their marriage had crumbled into the dust as fear became her prime emotion whenever he came near her. And so she had left him. Even the knowing looks she received from several people, who had tried to advise her to think carefully before marrying a man she barely knew, hadn't been enough to make her turn tail and go back for another try at the marriage. Her marriage had become an emotional torment she could no longer live with.

She had learnt months afterwards that Malcolm's behaviour—loving the whole world while he was winning, and blaming everyone else for his bad luck when he was losing, had been typical of all obsessive gamblers, that in fact he suffered from an illness, one that could have been treated, with his co-operation—something he would never have given!

It hadn't helped the situation that, following Sophie's departure from their flat, Malcolm began to win again! Not big wins, nothing near enough to pay off the crippling debts they still had, but enough to convince him he had been right about Sophie being the jinx in his life.

Not that Sophie had cared what he thought by that time; it was far too late to salvage anything from their marriage. And she was still trying to pay off all those debts they had acquired herself, feeling that one of them at least should make some effort to do so. And so she had found whatever work she could to support herself and make a start on paying some of the bills, knowing that there was no way her parents could help her, that it was up to her to get herself out of this mess.

And she had done it, for the main part, had organised
her life now in such a way that she slowly paid off those
mountainous debts while at the same time being able to
continue with her Open University course. It wasn't a
perfect arrangement by any means, but it was better than
a lot of people managed in her position, and, last of all,
it was the best she could do.

And now, for reasons of his own, Maximilian Grant
had thrown the whole thing back up in her face like some
avenging spectre!

Well, she wasn't going to sit here and wallow in self-
pity; she had her packing to do, and a train to catch,
she decided determinedly as she got to her feet. The
sooner she got herself moving, the better.

The only trouble was, she realised once her packing
was complete, was that the red T-shirt and denims she
had worn to go riding, and since thrown in the machine
to be washed, were still downstairs in the washing
machine, very damp too, no doubt. Which was just too
bad, because her wardrobe wasn't extensive enough for
her to just leave the two items behind. She would just
have to put them in a plastic carrier bag and take them
with her that way.

It was the final blow in an already traumatic day to
find, after quietly making her way to the laundry-room,
that tangled up with her T-shirt and denims were two of
Maximilian Grant's white shirts. At least . . . she presumed the shirts had once been white. But they certainly
weren't any longer.

The red colour from her cheaply bought T-shirt had
obviously run, and the white shirts were now a lovely
shade of pink!

CHAPTER SEVEN

SOPHIE'S first thoughts were ones of horror and panic! Would this catalogue of disasters which seemed to have been dogging her since she had arrived here never cease?

And then she tried to reason with herself that perhaps she hadn't dyed the shirts at all, maybe they had been pink to start with. Maximilian, in a pink shirt? Not just one, but two, in exactly the same shade? It didn't seem very likely. How about Paul Wiseman, then? That seemed even more unlikely. The other man's choice of clothing was even more conservative than Maximilian's had been. Besides, Paul Wiseman had only arrived this morning; it wasn't very likely that one of the first things he had done was throw two shirts into the washing machine!

No, she finally realised heavily, she would just have to accept that she had dyed two of Maximilian Grant's expensive—probably silk, knowing her luck!—shirts a glorious shade of pink!

Actually, she acknowledged with growing hysteria, as dyes went, she had done rather a good job! The colour wasn't patchy or faded, but a beautiful all-over bright pink that could have been achieved professionally. Not that she thought Maximilian would appreciate that fact, or indeed that he would ever want the colour professionally introduced to his shirts!

She heard a noise in the adjoining kitchen, hurriedly bundling the shirts inside her red T-shirt before tucking the crumpled bundle under her arm, forcing a bright smile to her lips as she marched forcefully into the kitchen, her bravado deflating somewhat when she saw it was May, not her aunt, who was moving efficiently about the kitchen. She couldn't believe that something had gone right at last, that she had a brief reprieve from Aunt Millie! It would only be a brief one, to be sure, but anything was better than nothing.

May gave her a startled look at the big beaming smile Sophie bestowed on her, hastily busying herself with the pie she was about to put in the oven.

Sophie's good luck seemed to be continuing as she made it back to her bedroom without meeting anyone else.

But she almost collapsed from shock when she turned, after closing the door quietly behind her, to find Maximilian sitting calmly on the side of her bed!

The bundle of clothes she carried fell unheeded to the floor, Sophie's hands moving up protectively even as she gasped her surprise at finding him there.

'I'm sorry.' Maximilian stood up slowly, silver-blue eyes narrowed on the paleness of her face. 'I didn't mean to startle you.'

Sophie recovered quickly. After all, this was his house; he was at liberty to go where he pleased in it. She just hadn't expected him to want to come to the bedroom he knew she had been allocated. Unless—her mouth tightened—he had come to make sure she went.

'Well, you did,' she snapped accusingly, grabbing up the damp clothing from the floor and dropping them down on to the bed—those pink shirts, thankfully, still rolled up inside her T-shirt!

His mouth thinned at the impatience of her rebuke. 'I did apologise,' he rasped in a hard voice.

'So you did.' Her mouth twisted. 'And I suppose I should feel grateful for that——'

'I realise you probably have a right to feel resentful, Sophie,' he sighed. 'But——'

'Do you?' Her eyes flashed deeply hazel. 'Believe me, Mr Grant, there's no probably about it! It's a very—nauseating experience, learning that your life has been put under someone else's microscope—and found wanting!'

'There was a good reason for that!' he put in defensively, a nerve pulsing in his tightly clenched jaw.

'I'm sure there was,' Sophie scorned. 'I wonder just how close a scrutiny your *own* life would bear without——'

'We aren't discussing me,' he told her stiffly.

'That's just the sort of reasoning that disgusts me!'

Maximilian's nostrils flared angrily, his eyes as cold as ice. 'You know nothing about it!'

'I know that I judge a person on what I find them to be, not on what some cold-blooded report tells me about them,' she challenged.

Every muscle and sinew seemed to be tensed with furious tension as Maximilian watched her with narrowed eyes. 'Cold-blooded,' he repeated in a silkily soft voice. 'Is that what you consider me?'

Sophie's own anger faltered slightly as she sensed a sudden change in his manner. There was something . . .

'Oh!' she gasped as she was suddenly pulled up against the hard length of his body, the warmth of his hands against the base of her spine. At that moment he felt anything but cold! 'Mr Grant——'

'Max or Maximilian,' he told her huskily. 'Don't try and put a distance between us with formality.'

Distance between them? A wisp of air would have difficulty getting in between them at this moment, their bodies were moulded so closely together! He had to stop doing this . . . !

'Maximilian.' She shook her head. 'I don't think——'

'I've been trying very hard not to since the moment you joined us for lunch wearing these!' His hands moved caressingly down the length of her hips and thighs in the body-hugging black leggings. 'You have the most fantastic legs . . . ! And you look sexy as hell in these things,' he added with a heartfelt groan.

Jennie's phraseology exactly, telling Sophie where the young girl had learnt such language!

But Jennie, quite frankly, was the last thing on her mind at this moment, every nerve-ending attuned to the sensuality of this man. Her breath came in short ragged gasps, hazel-coloured eyes a deep green as she gazed up at him.

'I need this!' Maximilian suddenly groaned, his head swooping down as his lips claimed hers, a sensual onslaught that almost swept Sophie off her feet.

His mouth tasted, teased, delighted in the moist promise of her lips, his arms tightening about her as his tongue probed silkily across her lips and then into the hot moisture of her mouth. Even her teeth seemed sensitised to the caress as pleasure coursed down her spine.

Muscles rippled beneath her fingertips as she clung to him. Maximilian's arms tightened about her, and Sophie felt him shudder against her at the caress of her fingertips down the column of his spine, heated passion engulfing her, engulfing them both as Maximilian's mouth returned to hers again and again, until Sophie wasn't even sure she was breathing any more, couldn't think, couldn't do anything but respond to his demand.

But she needed to breathe, and she surfaced for air, drawing deep ragged breaths into her starved lungs, her face feeling hot and flushed, her eyes feverish, every part of her straining even closer to Maximilian.

'You taste wonderful,' he murmured raggedly against the silky length of her throat, lips and tongue probing there, sending shivers of delight through her whole body. 'Milk and honey; pure nectar!'

All her senses were attuned to him too; taste, feel, look, smell, hearing. They were the only two people in the world at this moment, wanting and wanted, driven by a need now that was threatening to explode out of the control of either of them.

'God!' Maximilian's forehead was slightly damp as he rested it against hers, his breathing laboured, his arms tight about Sophie's waist, making her fully aware of his throbbing desire. 'I want you, Sophie,' he told her unnecessarily. 'I want you very badly!'

They had met for the first time only yesterday, event-filled as the time since might have been, and although Sophie ached for Maximilian in return she knew it was too soon for her to really know what she was doing. There had been no other men for her since the failure of her marriage to Malcolm, and he had been her first ever lover; by now Sophie knew herself well enough to realise she couldn't just jump into bed with a man because she desired him; she had probably desired Malcolm once, and look what a disaster that had turned out to be! She needed time to make sure she wouldn't be making just such another mistake now, with Maximilian.

And as she was leaving in a few minutes, there would never be that time...

Maximilian was looking down at her now with darkened eyes. 'I didn't expect anything like this to happen between us either, Sophie,' he grated as he saw the refusal in her expression, his jaw tightly clenched. 'I only came in here to ask you to stay on——'

'Again?' Sophie stepped back with a gasp, staring up at him incredulously. 'I don't believe you.' She shook her head dazedly. 'What happened to change your mind this time?' she scorned. 'Something Jennie said? Or was it what happened between us just now——'

'I told you, I came in here to ask you to stay on—and that was *before* I kissed you!' Maximilian bit out tautly, his eyes glittering dangerously.

Her mouth tightened. 'Then it was Jennie again,' she said disgustedly. 'What did she do this time, come into your study, stamp her foot a little, and demand——?'

'If you think back to our earlier conversation, Sophie, I told you then that I wasn't asking you to leave,' he reminded coldly.

And then he had kissed her... 'But you didn't actually try to stop me going,' she accused.

'Because I hadn't realised that, being you, you would come straight to your room then and there, pack your things and just go!' he returned icily.

Minutes ago they had been on the precipice of becoming lovers, now they faced each other almost as adversaries, both breathing deeply in their agitation, their bodies tense still, but with anger now, Maximilian's hands tightly clenched at his sides. It was an utterly ridiculous situation, Sophie suddenly realised.

She forced herself to take deep, calming breaths, some of the tension starting to leave her. 'What else did you think I could do?' she sighed heavily. 'You and that report had laid my life bare——'

'I realise that,' Maximilian groaned. 'Which was why I intended leaving you for a while before I explained that the report didn't actually change any opinion I had already formed of you,' he told her enigmatically—because he obviously had no intention, at this moment, of enlarging on that statement! 'God, considering the circumstances of your marriage, and your husband's—death, it was perfectly understandable that you chose to go back to your maiden name. Although,' his eyes narrowed again, 'you weren't completely honest about that, either, were you?'

She swallowed hard, moistening dry lips; as she had already said, that report had laid her *whole* life bare. 'I——'

The door suddenly burst open without warning and Jennie bounced into the room; thank God it hadn't been a few minutes earlier was Sophie's immediate thought.

'Well?' Jennie looked at her father eagerly. 'Is she staying?'

He glared at her at the intrusion. 'Jennifer——'

'*Lady* Sophie Gordon!' Jennie ignored her father, looking at Sophie admiringly. 'How absolutely marvellous!' She beamed her excitement at the revelation. 'Why didn't you tell me your father and mother are an earl and countess?' she added poutingly. 'Really, Sophie—or should I call you Lady Sophie now . . . ?' She frowned thoughtfully. 'I suppose really I——'

'I'm sure that if Sophie could get a word in edgeways she might be able to answer at least one of your impertinent questions,' her father cut in with icy derision.

Jennie looked as if she was about to argue the validity of this accusation, but, seeing the danger signs clearly evident in her father's expression, she seemed to think better of it, clamping her lips together, although her expression remained mutinous.

Sophie was glad of the few seconds' respite, felt as if she had been bombarded with thousands of tiny missiles—all of them hitting the target!

Lady Sophie Gordon. Yes, that was her. But the title, without the wealth to support it, was meaningless. During that final argument with Malcolm, he had cruelly told her her title was one of the main reasons he had married her, that 'my wife, Lady Sophie' had given him entrance to places he hadn't previously been able to get into, and 'my mother and father-in-law, the earl and countess' had given him a credibility that had fooled even more people. Obviously none of those people had been aware of the fact that the earl and countess barely managed to exist at all on the meagre payment her father could earn from the books he had written on archaeology, that there had never been any money there for luxuries.

The two sisters, Millie and Mary, had both 'gone into service' while still in their teens, both of them working then for the previous earl and countess, Sophie's grandparents. Even then there had been very little money, and the earl and countess had been absolutely horrified when their only son had fallen in love with the maid and announced his intention of marrying her! But, other than the actual title, Humphrey hadn't had a lot to offer one of the women of his so-called class. And anyway, he had made up his mind; he intended marrying Mary with or without his parents' approval.

Actually Mary's family, including her sister Millie, hadn't been any more keen for the marriage to take place; after all, Mary *was* the maid. A case of reverse snobbery!

But they had married, and against all odds the marriage was a happy one, although Sophie, born two years after they married, had remained their only child. But, if the marriage was a happy one, her grandparents' other prediction, about their ending up living in virtual poverty, had proved correct. Sophie's childhood very spartan, certainly no money for servants now, or a private education for Sophie.

But Malcolm hadn't cared about any of that, had married her for the title alone, loving the prestige he thought it gave him to have married into a titled family.

It was ironic that he should have felt that way, really, because with maturity Sophie had come to realise that half the attraction to Malcolm at that stage in her life had been the fact that he seemed to have all the advantages of money that had been so lacking all her life. She had been young, and stupid, and learnt her lesson the hard way.

In fact, such had been her lesson that she was attracted to Maximilian now *in spite of* his money!

Maximilian's gaze narrowed on her probingly now, as if he was trying to fathom her thoughts, finally shrugging defeat as she looked back at him calmly, turning to his daughter with sharp disapproval now. 'This is Sophie's bedroom for the duration of her stay,' he bit out reprovingly. 'You could at least have knocked before bursting in here.'

'But I did,' Jennie protested with an indignant pout.

Colour instantly heated Sophie's cheeks as she realised exactly *why* she and Maximilian hadn't heard that knock!

'Then maybe it would have been more polite to have waited outside until you were asked to come in.' She spoke more sharply than she had intended, instantly feeling guilty for it as Jennie looked hurt at the rebuke. 'It would have been the polite thing to do, Jennie,' she added in a gentler tone.

'Sorry,' the disgruntled teenager muttered.

Maximilian's eyes widened at this acquiescence, grudgingly given as it was, turning to Sophie with speculative eyes before turning back to Jennie. 'Maybe we'll have more luck if *you* ask Sophie to stay on?' he suggested drily.

Sophie glared at him protestingly for his astuteness; he wasn't playing fair. He had guessed that she felt a sort of reverse affinity with Jennie, the young girl the result of a wealthy and privileged background, Sophie the product of an impoverished titled one—both disadvantages in their own way.

'Sophie knows I want her to stay,' Jennie muttered awkwardly, her expression rebellious now.

Asking for anything didn't come easy to this young girl, Sophie was already aware of that. But that wasn't the problem now. If it were only Jennie she had to consider... But the truth of the matter was, after this most recent time in Maximilian's arms, she was no longer sure staying here would be a good idea. It would give her that valuable time to get to know him...!

'Please,' Jennie added abruptly when she saw Sophie was about to refuse.

Neither member of this family played fair, Sophie realised with an inward groan. How could she possibly refuse this young girl, when she knew how much it had cost her to almost plead in that way?

But she was almost tempted to do just that when she looked up and caught the blaze of triumph in Maximilian's eyes as he sensed her capitulation to Jennie's plea! Although she knew she couldn't disappoint Jennie just because of Maximilian and the way she responded to him. Or the way he responded to her! But she wasn't about to give in as easily as he thought she was...

A glint of mischief sparkled in her eyes. 'There's something else I ought to tell your father before I accept——'

'You accept!' Jennie pounced gleefully, the sulky expression gone instantly. 'That's——'

'Hold on, Jennie—once I've made this final admission, your father may not want me to,' Sophie kept her expression deliberately deadpan, although she was sure there was merriment dancing in her eyes; if Maximilian didn't want to play fair, neither would she!

Maximilian watched her warily, obviously sensing some sort of trap. 'Yes?' he slowly prompted with suspicion.

Sophie moved to the bed, her mocking gaze never leaving his face as she bent to pick up the damp T-shirt, triumphantly producing the two pink shirts from inside

it. 'Yours, I believe!' She held them up aloft so that the
vividness of the pink shade should be seen in all its glory.

He frowned his puzzlement, shaking his head. 'I don't
have any pink shirts.'

Jennie moved to look more closely at the two shirts,
lightly touching the red of the T-shirt too. 'You do now!'
she realised. 'How priceless!' she chuckled. 'Sophie obviously washed your shirts in with her T-shirt, and the
colour ran!'

For a brief moment Maximilian continued to look be-
mused, and then his mouth twitched, before he began
to chuckle in earnest, his eyes crinkling up at the corners,
his laughter a deep husky sound in his chest. 'Jennie's
right.' He shook his head in rueful amusement. 'You are
priceless!'

Anyone looking at the three of them, Sophie grinning,
Jennie and Maximilian openly laughing, and over the
fact that Maximilian now possessed two perfectly dyed
pink shirts he was never going to wear, could be forgiven
for thinking they were all a little mad. But it was the
release of tension, as much as anything else, that was
causing their amusement—as Sophie had hoped that it
might—and so they could possibly be forgiven for over-
reacting to the triviality. Although Sophie hadn't thought
it was trivial when she first discovered what had
happened!

Maximilian's mouth twisted ruefully. 'Well, as I have
no intention of starting to wear pink shirts, they may as
well be disposed of!'

'Certainly not!' Sophie gasped, scandalised at his
casual dismissal of such obviously expensive items. 'I
could wear them as nightshirts——' She broke off awkwardly, her cheeks burning with colour, at the sudden
hunger in Maximilian's eyes. 'Er—or perhaps Mr
Wiseman would wear them?' she hastily suggested,

totally flustered by Maximilian's reaction to the thought of her going to bed in his shirts.

'Paul?' Maximilian looked more amused than ever. 'Does he look like a man who would wear pink shirts either?' he derided.

'Now that you mention it, no!' Sophie grimaced. 'I really am very sor——'

'Paul...' Jennie repeated in a puzzled voice. 'Sophie keeps mentioning his name, but—who on earth is he, Daddy?' she frowned. 'Some good-looking young businessman you've brought down with you for the weekend?' she prompted eagerly.

Blond brows rose over rueful blue eyes. 'You are growing up, aren't you?' her father said. 'You used to refer to them as stuffy old businessmen who took up far too much of my time! Well, I'm sorry to disappoint you,' he shrugged. 'But Paul works for me. As for his being good-looking... Perhaps Sophie could answer that better than me?' His gaze was narrowed on her speculatively.

But Jennie, obviously still puzzled even by this explanation for the other man's presence here, saved Sophie the embarrassment of having to answer that question. 'He works for you...?' Jennie repeated sharply. 'But what's happened to Uncle Sean? He's been with us—you, for years, and——'

'Calm down, love,' her father cut in soothingly. 'Sean still works for me; he should be driving down on Monday to join us, he's just—dealing with a few last-minute details in London that couldn't be left for the week. Paul is—helping out. For a few weeks,' he dismissed with a shrug.

'But——'

'Jennie, would you like to help me unpack—yet again?' Sophie drawled—although in actual fact she was only trying to help divert Jennie's attention away from questioning her father in the way that she was;

Maximilian was obviously tiring of it, his patience starting to wear a little thin as his answers became more and more terse. In actual fact, Sophie doubted he was used to having his decisions questioned by anyone. 'And then we can go down to the tennis-court I saw over behind the stables earlier,' she suggested lightly, although by the feel of it, the muscles she had used for the unaccustomed ride she had taken this afternoon were already starting to stiffen up, and would no doubt protest painfully at a game of tennis. But she was here to keep Jennie entertained and busy, and the young girl looked as if she was already anticipating the game. 'I should warn you,' Sophie hastened to add as her body felt like protesting already, 'it's years since I played!'

Jennie frowned. 'But surely as Lady Sophie——'

'Don't keep prying into Sophie's private life, Jennifer,' her father rasped. 'I'm sure if she wants to tell you about it, she will.'

Sophie looked at him gratefully, aware that he already knew all about her private life, albeit from that damned report. And she would tell Jennie some of it, at least the part about being 'Lady' Sophie; the young girl was going to find it was far from romantic!

Maximilian moved across the room. 'Another thing——' He paused in the doorway. 'Paul isn't the only—new employee you'll see about the place… Maybe you will find one of them is good-looking,' he added drily. 'But if you leave the house for any reason, to go to the stables, or to the tennis-courts, I want you to let someone know about it——'

'What on earth for?' Jennie complained. 'Really, Daddy, aren't you taking all this a little too——?'

'All what?' her father rasped tautly, his body tense, eyes narrowed to icy blue slits.

'I was only thinking about the good-looking business associate!' Jennie's face flushed with anger. 'You don't have to make sure I'm chaperoned at all times,' she snapped. 'I don't intend eloping with the first presentable man I see!' she added disgustedly.

Maximilian's mouth set tightly. 'Just make sure that you don't leave the house without telling someone where you're going!' he repeated coldly before leaving the room, the door closing forcefully behind him.

Sophie stared after him in dismay. For a short time—a very short time, it transpired!—there had been a rapport between father and daughter, a rapport that had been utterly destroyed by the way he had suddenly turned into the autocratic father seconds ago, determined to keep his daughter protected—even if she didn't want to be!

There had to be a reason for his being like this, but without knowing more of the background, possibly more about Jennie's mother, Sophie couldn't hope to fathom it out. What she did know was that it wasn't wise to try to cage up a headstrong girl like Jennie. It was sure to lead to trouble...

CHAPTER EIGHT

'So WHERE the hell is she?' Maximilian was white with anger as he glared down at Sophie.

And nothing Sophie said was going to make him look—or for that matter feel—any differently! Because she didn't know any more than he where Jennie was. Although...she could probably take a not too inaccurate guess...

Despite her forebodings, after Maximilian's arrogant issue of orders on Saturday, and Jennie's obvious rebellious reaction to this autocratic behaviour, the rest of that day and Sunday had passed smoothly enough. Too smoothly, it now seemed, because it was only one o'clock on this bright and sunny Monday and Jennie was apparently nowhere to be found.

And Maximilian was absolutely furious about it. With good reason, Sophie had to admit, even if she hadn't been particularly keen on the way he summoned her and demanded to know of Jennie's whereabouts, just as if she really were Jennie's gaoler, which she had no intention of being. But, to give him his due, Maximilian had issued few instructions for their behaviour during this week, only two really, the rule about telling someone if they left the house, and also that they should not be late for meals. And as they all knew lunch was at twelve-thirty, and they had already spent half an hour looking for the young girl when she hadn't come to the dining-room that time, Jennie had broken both those requests in one go. Because she certainly wasn't in the house either!

Sean McKay had arrived this morning, and Jennie had greeted him ecstatically, obviously pleased to see again the man she called Uncle Sean. And Sophie had to admit he was a likeable man, in his early fifties, tall, with iron-grey hair that he kept styled short, with warm grey eyes set in a craggily handsome face. He had never married, Jennie had informed her, had made his work for Maximilian his life, and Maximilian's family his own. Which made Jennie's earlier fear, that he might have been replaced, more understandable. It was because of Jennie's obvious closeness to the man, who behaved towards her more like a grandfather than an uncle, that Sophie had believed the young girl when she'd told her earlier this morning that she was going down to the study to talk to Sean for a while. She obviously hadn't done any such thing, and, from Sophie's calculations of when Jennie had supposedly gone to see Sean, the young girl had been missing for over two hours!

'You were supposed to be with her at all times,' Maximilian continued with hard accusation. 'Why didn't you——?'

'Calm down, Max,' Sean cut in softly, smoothly. 'I'm sure none of this is Sophie's fault——'

'Are you?' his employer and friend scorned. 'Nothing seems to have gone right since she arrived here! I——'

'Sophie's arrival coincided with Jennie's own,' Sean pointed out reasoningly, shooting Sophie a sympathetic smile, obviously having no idea of the way in which Sophie and Maximilian had first met. 'And we both of us know how determined *that* young lady can be!' Sean added indulgently, shaking his head ruefully. 'I'm sure Sophie did her best——'

'It obviously wasn't good enough!' Maximilian rasped accusingly, his hands clenching into fists at his sides as he turned away frustratedly.

Sophie felt awful for the obvious distress he was going through, and knew, too, that she was responsible. For all that she and Jennie seemed to have been developing a friendship, Jennie being absolutely fascinated by the 'poor Lady Sophie', Sophie herself had suspected that something like this might happen from the time Maximilian had issued the arrogant instruction about not leaving the house without telling someone first. Jennie's exemplary behaviour yesterday had obviously lulled Sophie into a false sense of security, the distraction of Sean's arrival this morning being all she had needed to make good her escape!

'I believe,' she began tentatively, 'that Jennie may have gone into town shopping——'

'Shopping!' Maximilian repeated incredulously, turning round from glaring stony-faced out of the bay window in the sitting-room, where they had all congregated when Jennie had failed to arrive for lunch as expected.

Sophie winced at the cold glitter of his eyes as his gaze pinned her remorselessly to the spot. 'She suggested we go into town this morning,' she explained with an uncomfortable shrug. 'But I thought the afternoon might be a better time, and so I——'

'You thought?' Maximilian repeated silkily soft. 'You aren't paid to *think*, *Lady* Sophie——'

'Max, really, there's no need for that,' Sean cut in placatingly at the deliberate insult, his years with Maximilian, and their obvious friendship, giving him— he seemed to feel, at least—that right.

Both Sophie and Maximilian ignored his reproach. 'I haven't been paid at all yet, Mr Grant!' Sophie glared at him, fists on her hips in challenge. 'And if not being allowed to think for oneself is part of the condition of working for you, then I think I would rather not bother!'

'Not again!' Maximilian rolled his eyes expressively. 'You really are the most ridiculous young——'

'*I'm* ridiculous?' she scorned incredulously. 'Your reaction to Jennie's having slipped off alone for a couple of hours shopping is really over the top,' she accused heatedly. 'Maybe if you hadn't issued that stupid order in the first place she wouldn't have felt the need to challenge your authority! She hasn't run off with the gardener or anything,' Sophie shook her head impatiently. 'Good God, the man is seventy if he's a day! And those other "new employees" you told us about are all middle-aged.' She and Jennie had seen several of the men about the place, but they hadn't spoken to them, and, as far as Sophie was aware, Jennie hadn't spoken to any of them either. 'That only leaves Paul,' she derided. 'Perhaps she's run off with him!' It was true that the other man wasn't in here with them now, but, to give him his due, he had been earlier when the search had first begun. But if Maximilian could behave in this ludicrously unreasonable way, so could she!

He looked ready to explode. 'You——'

'Max, tempers are becoming more than a little frayed,' Sean cut in softly. 'Maybe if you explained everything to Sophie she might——'

'Yes—why don't you "explain everything to Sophie"!' She glared at Maximilian. 'Instead of acting like some Victorian father in a melodrama——'

'I am *reacting* like a man concerned for his daughter's welfare!' he attacked in return.

'Maybe if Sophie had known all the facts,' Sean began again placatingly—and it was easy to see in that moment how he had lasted so long as Maximilian's employee; he obviously liked and respected the younger man, and that liking and respect was reciprocated—otherwise Sean would have been sacked long ago for his impertinence in interfering in family concerns, tactfully as it was being done!

'She didn't need to know anything!' Maximilian turned on Sean too now, eyes glittering coldly, dangerously so.

'I'm probably not paid to *know* anything either, Sean,' Sophie sighed heavily. Her head was spinning from the tension that seemed to actually be crackling in the air. And it was Maximilian who was creating this totally out of context reaction. At least . . . she presumed it was out of context, although from the little that had been said between the two men there was obviously something that Maximilian wasn't telling her—that he had no intention of telling her either! 'Maybe if we all——' She broke off as the door burst open.

But it wasn't Jennie who had entered, as they had all hoped it might be when they turned so eagerly towards the doorway, the anticipation quickly turning to disappointment when they saw it was only Paul who stood there.

He didn't spare Sophie and Sean so much as a second glance, his face grim as he looked at Maximilian. 'Gracious Lady has gone too!' he bit out abruptly. 'I've just checked with Jenkins, and the horse's stall is empty. I can't emphasise too deeply how strongly I advised you that something exactly like this could happen——'

'I don't think I-told-you-sos are in order just now, Wiseman,' Sean rasped harshly, his worried gaze returning to Maximilian's ashen face. 'Max only did what he thought was best. For everyone concerned,' Sean added with emphasis. 'The fact that it hasn't worked out that way certainly isn't his fault.'

Sophie didn't know why they were still making such a fuss about this. It was perfectly obvious to her what had happened now that she knew the horse was missing too; Jennie obviously loved the beautiful animal, had lingered in the horse's stall yesterday morning before they went riding, obviously itching to get up on the filly's back, prevented from doing so, Sophie had presumed, because the horse obviously belonged to Maximilian personally. But obviously today Jennie hadn't been able to resist the temptation, going off on Lady—Gracious Lady—without telling anyone. She couldn't tell anyone, had known she wouldn't be allowed to ride the horse at all if she did that. Why none of these men could see that, Sophie didn't know!

'I realise Jennie shouldn't have been late back for lunch,' she began with rueful affection; obviously Jennie was so enjoying her ride she had completely forgotten the time. 'And I'm sure by now she does too!' Sophie grimaced. No doubt Jennie had realised by now that she had lost track of time and broken one of her father's two rules, and her initial panic would probably have turned to defiance by now too. Sophie only wished she could get to the young girl first and advise her that a contrite apology for her behaviour would probably get a sweeter reaction than rebellion. Although Sophie wouldn't guarantee it, not the way Maximilian looked at the moment! 'But no doubt she'll be here in a few minutes, and then we can all——'

'What are you burbling on about?' Maximilian turned on her fiercely, a white line of tension about the firmness of his mouth, his jaw clenched in tight control. 'Haven't you realised yet that Jennifer hasn't just gone off on some shopping spree at all——?'

'Of course I've realised that,' Sophie sharply interrupted his derisive scorn. 'But I don't happen to think her having borrowed your horse to go riding necessitates a lynch mob either! And anyone more like a lynch mob than you three I have yet to see!' She looked at the men with incredulity. 'Don't you think you should lighten up a little?' she attempted to cajole them. 'At least give the poor girl a chance to defend herself when she gets back——'

'She may not be coming back!' Maximilian's voice rose with frustrated anger.

Sophie frowned 'Of course she will,' she soothed. 'Jennie is a very good rider. I know Gracious Lady is obviously a spirited animal, but I'm sure Jennie can handle her.' The young girl was an excellent horse-woman. Almost as good as her father, Sophie had realised early this morning when she looked out of her bedroom window and saw Maximilian returning to the stable from his ride. But not on the back of Gracious Lady, she recalled now... And, considering what a beautifully spirited animal the horse was, she could probably have done with the exercise. Maximilian should really be thanking Jennie for saving him the trouble of taking Gracious Lady out, not berating her!

'And just what would you know about it?' Maximilian demanded aggressively now.

Once again he was deliberately insulting, and Sophie couldn't help bristling indignantly. 'I realise you're upset about Jennie's disappearance, Mr Grant,' she began coolly. 'But I really don't think insulting me is——'

'Oh, for God's sake don't start thinking again!' he scorned harshly. 'You don't have any idea what you're talking about——'

'What's all the shouting about?'

This time, it *was* Jennie standing in the doorway, when they all spun around. But there was no eager expectation in any of their faces this time; a rueful greeting in Sophie's, restrained relief on the part of Sean and Paul—and furious disbelief from Maximilian as he looked at his daughter with incredulity.

And, from the defiant expression on Jennie's own face as she met his gaze, there would be no joyful reunion between father and daughter; in fact, the fur looked as if it was about to start flying!

Jennie strolled completely into the room, dressed, as Sophie had guessed she would be, in her dark green riding-jacket, fawn jodhpurs tucked into black dust-covered boots, her long hair tied back at her nape with a dark green velvet ribbon, the golden mane cascading down her spine.

'Did someone die?' she drawled when no one seemed in any hurry to answer her first question, her brows arched in derisive query.

'No,' her father answered her softly. 'But "someone" is about to!' He took a threatening step towards her, only to have Sean put a restraining hand on his arm.

The coldly furious glare he shot the other man was enough to make Sean remove his hand, but the few seconds' delay in Maximilian's reaching Jennie had had the desired effect; he no longer looked ready to strangle his daughter without hearing. First he would get an explanation from her, *then* he would strangle her, Sophie realised with a grimace!

'Where the hell have you been, Jennifer?' he demanded to know with forceful intent, his hands clenched at his sides. Probably so that he shouldn't put them around his daughter's throat—yet!

'Perhaps we should all leave and let you two—talk,' Sophie suggested helpfully, sure there was no need for them all to witness Jennie's humiliation. Because she didn't doubt for one moment that that was what it was going to be; Maximilian didn't look as if he was about to be talked round this time!

'No,' he said now in a tone that brooked no argument, Sean and Paul slowly turning back uncertainly from where they had been about to leave. 'We've all been sent on a wild-goose chase looking for this inconsiderate young lady the last hour, so we *all* deserve the explanation. And apology.' This last was added in a way that should have warned Jennie that that was the least he expected of her.

Whether or not she chose to heed that warning was another matter entirely! From the rebellious flush that darkened her cheeks, Sophie didn't think so.

There she went, thinking again! As if sensing her self-derision, Maximilian turned to look at her with narrowed eyes. Oh, dear, he looked ready to kill!

He turned back to his daughter. 'Well?'

'OK, so I'm a little late for lunch,' she began dismissively.

'And you took Gracious Lady without telling anyone,' her father pointed out softly, dangerously so.

'Ah.' Jennie chewed on her top lip ruefully. 'You know about that too,' she grimaced.

'Of course we——' Maximilian paused to draw in a deep ragged breath, controlling his outburst with difficulty. 'And no matter what you might think to the contrary, you aren't an experienced enough rider to handle a horse like Gracious Lady,' he grated. 'Anything could have happened!'

Jennie's eyes flashed icy blue. 'You mean I may have damaged your precious horse with my inept handling of her?' she scorned defiantly. 'Well, she's safe enough. If you don't believe me, go out to the stables and see for yourself!' She ran to the door, her intention to flee from the room obvious to them all.

'Jennie!' Sophie called to her encouragingly. 'I'm sure your father didn't mean that at all——'

'Are you?' the young girl derided pityingly. 'Then you don't know him very well! I've always come way down on his list of priorities.'

'Jennifer——'

'What's the matter, Daddy?' She looked at him as if she really hated him at that moment—something Sophie knew just wasn't true. In actual fact, Jennie adored her father, looked up to him, and her constant goading of him was just a defence mechanism because for some reason Jennie believed her love wasn't returned. 'Don't you like having an audience to the truth about the way you feel about me?' Jennie challenged now. 'It's your audience, Daddy,' she scorned. '*You* ordered them to stay here and listen to this. It's your own fault if you don't like what they're hearing! And the truth is that you couldn't really give a damn about me, that all you care about is your precious horse. After all, on a business level—the only level you function on!—she's worth a lot more money than I am!'

'Jennifer, you're going too far!' Maximilian bit out in a perfectly controlled voice, but his face was pale none the less, a nerve pulsing in his cheek.

Sophie was sure Sean and Paul were in agreement with that, as she was herself, but all of them seemed frozen in this cameo, unable to bring it to an end.

'Because I'm telling you the truth but it's something you don't want to hear?' Jennie continued remorselessly. 'I never wanted to hear the rows between you and Mummy when I was younger. I never wanted to hear the words "boarding school," let alone be sent to one. And I certainly didn't ever want to hear the words "divorce" and "custody"!' Unshed tears glistened in her eyes as she hurled these painful memories at her father. 'But that last word didn't apply to you, did it?' Her anger returned, although her voice broke emotionally. 'You were quite willing to give Mummy custody of me—you just wanted both of us out of your life. What a pity for you that Mummy died before there could be a divorce!' She was breathing hard in her agitation.

Sophie looked concernedly at Maximilian, could see that he was absolutely stunned by this outburst, that, probably for the first time in his life, he was speechless. And no wonder. Jennie had obviously been harbouring a lot of resentment towards her father for a lot of years, even before her mother had died by the sound of it. She had believed Maximilian didn't want her at all.

Jennie must have her reasons for believing that, and yet Sophie was sure Maximilian genuinely cared about his daughter...

'What a pity for you!' Jennie repeated scathingly when he gave no answer to the accusation, turning on her heel and running from the room.

It was then that Sophie saw, that they *all* saw as they watched Jennie's departure with pained expressions on their faces, that Jennie hadn't returned alone, that she had brought someone back with her, someone Sophie recognised only too well—Brian! And he had just been witness to a very private conversation between Maximilian and his daughter.

Private enough to give him a very good story to sell to a national newspaper...!

But before Sophie could gather her scattered wits together enough to say anything—although quite what she could have said, she had no idea—Maximilian had crossed the room in long aggressive strides, standing over Brian now, much taller and broader than the younger man.

'Who the hell are you?' Maximilian demanded, coldly furious at finding a complete stranger standing in the hallway of his home.

Sophie couldn't exactly blame him for being annoyed. And he would be even more upset than he was if he knew Brian was a reporter...

As for Brian, he had the look of a man who had walked into a cage full of lions—and the door had just firmly closed behind him! 'Er—I was just on my way up to the house when I met Jennie outside,' he explained

hastily, shooting Sophie anxious looks, having no idea
what he had just said to further antagonise Maximilian
Grant, but knowing there was a flash of fresh anger in
those icy blue eyes at his statement.

Poor Brian could have no idea that it was his familiarity with Jennie's name that had further angered
Maximilian! At least, Sophie hoped that was what it was,
and not that Maximilian had recognised Brian as the
man from Friday night...

Maximilian watched the younger man with narrowed
eyes. 'And exactly why were you "on your way" to this
house at all?' he immediately confirmed—to Sophie's
immense relief!—that he hadn't recognised Brian. Not
yet, anyway... 'I don't know you—do I...?' he added
slowly, Brian's voice perhaps striking a memory for him.

Brian shot Sophie another pleading look, obviously
deeply regretting now whatever impulse had encouraged
him to come here at all. Or at least making the mistake
of revealing his presence this way in the hallway; Sophie
very much doubted that Brian actually regretted being
privy to that very revealing scene between father and
daughter. And the sooner she talked to him about *that*,
the better!

'Brian is—a friend of mine,' she put in hastily. 'You
should have telephoned first, Brian.' The glare she gave
him utterly belied the pleasantness of her tone. 'I would
have met you in town,' she added pointedly.

'Brian...?' Maximilian repeated thoughtfully with a
dark frown, the memory he was searching for still
seeming to elude him.

But not for long, Sophie was sure. 'Come on, Brian,'
she took a firm hold of his arm. 'We'll go through to
the kitchen and see my aunt.'

'Brian...' Maximilian repeated to himself again, the
upset with Jennie obviously having deprived him of his

usual astuteness. But not for long, if Sophie knew him at all!

'Excuse us,' she said to no one in particular, dragging Brian from the room. Not that he wanted to linger, realising his mistake by now in having revealed his presence there at all. But Sophie thanked God he had; she would have the chance to issue dire warnings to him now about the inadvisability of using any of what he had just heard to further his career. It would just have the opposite effect if Maximilian was to turn nasty!

What Sophie actually wanted to do was go to Jennie, but at the moment talking to Brian was more urgent; she would use threats on him if necessary.

'Don't even bother to ask,' he warned as they stopped outside the kitchen and he saw the mutinous expression on her face.

'I'm not asking, Brian,' she told him steadily. 'I'm telling you that you can't use privileged information that you overheard by——'

'Don't be silly, Sophie,' he laughed dismissively, gaining in confidence by the minute now that he was away from Maximilian, a glowing excitement in his eyes now at the thought of the future opening up before him. 'It wasn't privileged at all, just a good old-fashioned family argument that I happened to overhear——'

'Between Mr Grant and his daughter,' she pointed out exasperatedly; they both knew Maximilian and Jennie weren't just any old family, that they were very newsworthy!

'It was very revealing,' Brian confirmed with a satisfied nod. 'What was even more interesting, though, was the horse Jennie was——'

'Sophie!' Her aunt spoke sharply as she came out of the kitchen at that moment and almost walked into them. 'Brian...?' she greeted with a disapproving frown.

He straightened with what looked like an almost guilty flush. 'I was just on my way to see you.'

'Through the main house?' She looked sceptical.

Sophie had to agree, it wasn't very convincing as a way of explaining his presence here; why on earth would he be on his way to see her aunt anyway?

'It just happened that way,' he shrugged dismissively. 'I actually came over to tell you I was talking to Arlette on the telephone last night, and she wanted me to come over and give you her love,' he explained smoothly. 'Of course I was delighted,' he added warmly. 'I know how much you've worried about her since she's been away, so I came over as soon as I could get away from work.'

Sophie frowned at his almost triumphant look in her direction, not understanding this at all. Why on earth would her cousin Arlette be telephoning Brian Burnett, rather than her own mother, all way way from Germany...?

'Arlette and I started dating a couple of months before she took the job in Germany,' Brian told her dismissively as he sat at the kitchen table drinking the mug of coffee Aunt Millie had poured for him, having thawed towards him completely at being given news of her daughter. Sophie wouldn't even have offered him any coffee, was still too upset with him because he obviously intended using that information he had about Jennie and Maximilian. She had no doubt he was going to use it to his own advantage.

But her aunt had seemed to forget completely his breach of etiquette in coming through the main house as he talked to her about her beloved daughter. She had poured them all a mug of coffee in the hope that she could persuade him to sit down and tell her all about the call while he drank it. But she had no sooner poured the coffee than she was rung for from the sitting-room, and had to hurry off to answer the call with mutterings about 'more comings and goings in this house lately than Piccadilly Circus'. Her departure had left the way clear for Sophie to sort things out with Brian once and for all.

The fact that she now knew he had been dating her cousin, prior to her going to Germany to work, explained a few things that had been puzzling Sophie. Aunt Millie's rather restrained reaction to knowing Brian was the 'friend' driving her home on Friday night, for one thing; her poor aunt had probably been horrified that she might be trying to steal her cousin's boyfriend while Arlette was away in Germany!

Brian's friendship with Arlette also explained his own sudden burst of ambition, after years of supposedly being quite content to sit back on his laurels in the provinces; Arlette was ambitious, had made no secret from childhood that she intended marrying well one day, had no intention of marrying and having children and living out the rest of her days in some backwater, struggling to make ends meet. Obviously Brian was trying to make sure he had more to offer Arlette than that, knowing he wouldn't stand a chance of making anything permanent out of the relationship if he didn't. Sophie knew it too. Fond of her cousin as she was, she was well aware that, when Arlette set her mind on a certain path, nothing would divert her from seeing it through—not even falling in love!

Yes, Sophie understood Brian's predicament a little better now, but she still had no intention of letting him use Maximilian and Jennie to further his career—even with the aim of winning the heart of her own cousin!

'That's very nice for you,' Sophie acknowledged distractedly. 'Very nice for you both. But we hadn't finished talking about Maximilian and Jennie——'

'Oh, but we had,' Brian stood up decisively. 'I'm not going to tell you I won't use the information, Sophie, because I have every intention of doing so——'

'Maximilian will probably sue you!' Sophie told him frustratedly.

'For what?' Brian scorned. 'For telling the truth? Look, I'm doing you a favour as it is, Sophie, almost being a member of the family, and all that,' he added with a slight flush to his cheeks.

'Doing me a favour?' she echoed incredulously. 'By getting me sacked? Because that's what will happen if you publish a story about Maximilian's—complicated, relationship with his daughter.' And she had already been sacked or resigned from this particular job enough times to last her a lifetime! 'You may even get Aunt Millie dismissed too,' she added with what she was sure was a stroke of genius; if he really was serious about his intentions towards Arlette, he certainly wouldn't want to get his possible future mother-in-law sacked as housekeeper here. Not that Sophie really believed it would come to that... After all, Maximilian believed Brian was here to see her, had no idea of that other family connection. But it wouldn't hurt for Brian to think it was a possibility!

Unfortunately, Brian was a lot brighter than she gave him credit for, because he just smiled confidently at the mere idea of her aunt being dismissed. 'I'm not about to advertise the fact that I'm dating Millie's daughter,' he derided. 'And I very much doubt that you are either!' And I *am* doing you a favour, Sophie,' he sobered with a frown. 'Because there's a much bigger story going on here than Grant's rocky relationship with his daughter...'

Sophie looked at him sharply. 'What on earth do you mean?'

'The horse, Sophie,' he said impatiently. 'The horse Jennie was riding when I met her outside,' he explained as Sophie still looked puzzled.

'Lady?' She frowned, still completely puzzled by the horse's significance.

'*Gracious* Lady,' Brian corrected pointedly. 'Oh, come on, Sophie,' he rebuked her shortly. 'It must have crossed your mind to wonder what a racehorse of that calibre is doing here rather than at its trainer's stables, let alone being ridden by Jennie Grant!'

Racehorse? That beautiful chestnut mare, the one she had almost saddled and ridden herself on Saturday, was a racehorse?

Sophie instantly visualised the chestnut mare; her smooth flowing lines, her excitability, the high charged power in her body—and she knew without a doubt that Brian was telling the truth: Lady—Gracious Lady—*was* a racehorse. She didn't know why she hadn't realised it before.

What *was* the horse doing here?

CHAPTER NINE

By the time she went upstairs a short time later, intending to talk to Jennie, Sophie had come up with any number of reasons why Gracious Lady should be here and not at the stables of her trainer. Maybe Maximilian had argued with the trainer and removed the horse from his stable? Maybe the horse was ill and needed to be kept from other racing horses? Maybe she was in a race locally during the next few days and it was easier to transport her from here?

There were all sorts of reasons, she had assured Brian, why Maximilian should have removed his own horse to his own home. She had told Brian that, knowing that she wasn't absolutely sure she believed it herself...

There were those rather enigmatic references Sean had made earlier, about something she should probably have known about, followed by Paul Wiseman's near panic at the fact that Gracious Lady had gone from her stable as well as Jennie from the house. No, the more she thought about it, the more convinced she was in her own mind that there was something more going on here than she knew about, something, as Brian so rightly pointed out, to do with Gracious Lady's presence here. But there was no way she was even going to give a hint of her own misgivings to Brian!

But no matter what she said to him, she wasn't able to convince him not to go ahead with that other story about Jennie and Maximilian. It was such a mess!

Jennie sat dry-eyed on top of her bed when Sophie entered the bedroom, although from the puffy look to her red-rimmed eyes she had been crying only minutes ago. Sophie ached to comfort her, but the fierce look Jennie gave her warned her against even trying.

'I'll come back later, shall I?' she suggested lightly. Jennie didn't even bother to answer her, lost in her misery once again.

Maximilian, it seemed, hadn't even bothered to come up and see his daughter; he couldn't have done, or Jennie wouldn't look the way she did!

After all that had been said earlier, and Jennie's obvious distress, Maximilian hadn't even come up here to reassure his daughter of his love for her. Well, Sophie didn't care if it got her sacked all over again; she was going to tell him exactly what she thought of his callousness.

Secretly, she knew, she was hoping there was a perfectly good reason for his not having been to see Jennie; she didn't want him to be the type of man who showed such a cold disregard of feelings towards his daughter's feelings. Because if he couldn't express love and understanding for his daughter, the one person he could love without fear of comeback, what possible chance did *any* woman have in his life...?

After years of feeling wary of men, Sophie knew she was falling in love with Maximilian, of all men!

When? How? *Why*? It was that last question that bothered her the most. She didn't need any emotional entanglements complicating her life, barely managed to keep all the different compartments of her life juggling at one go as it was. Falling in love, and so hopelessly, just played no part in her future plans.

But love was the last thing on her mind when she finally managed to locate Maximilian in the stables, talking soothingly to Gracious Lady as Jenkins brushed her down after her ride! Maximilian was comforting the horse, when it was Jennie he should be concerned with!

'What on earth do you think you're doing?' Sophie gasped disbelievingly, staring at him uncomprehendingly.

Maximilian looked round at her with cold blue eyes. 'I beg your pardon?'

Oh, no, he didn't—he wasn't going to get out of this by looking down his arrogant nose at her and in so doing putting her firmly in her place as companion to his daughter! It was because she was Jennie's friend, as well as her companion, that she was here at all. ''Your daughter is upstairs in her bedroom breaking her heart because she believes you love this horse more than you love her, and I come out here and find you consoling the stupid horse! No doubt assuring her you won't let the nasty girl up on her back again!' Sophie scorned accusingly.

'Would you leave us, Jenkins?' Maximilian instructed smoothly, waiting until the other man had left, prudently closing the stable door behind him as he went, before speaking again. 'Would you like to explain that statement?' He hadn't moved, standing very still, that very stillness threatening in itself.

'Isn't it self-explanatory?' Sophie sighed wearily, so disappointed in him.

He shook his head, his expression grim. 'I realise I behaved like a bastard towards you earlier, talking to you the way I did, and I apologise.' He shrugged dismissively.

Sophie couldn't believe he was this insensitive. She *knew* he wasn't this insensitive. 'Maximilian, why are you doing this?' She looked at him pleadingly, needing him to be different, to be the man she was falling in love with; she couldn't be this wrong about someone. About Maximilian...

Now he moved, crossing in front of the horse to grasp Sophie by the tops of her arms. 'Say that again,' he rasped.

She blinked up at him. 'Why are you doing this . . . ?'

'No!' He shook her none too gently. 'Say my name again! No one else has ever called me Maximilian. And I've so wanted you to.'

'You've . . . ?' She shook her head incredulously. 'Maximilian, you can't——' She broke off abruptly as his head bent, his lips dangerously close to hers.

'Can't what?' he murmured huskily against her throat.

She couldn't remember! It was so warm in here, smelt of soft sweet hay and that earthy smell of horses, was so basically primitive that—— Now she remembered! 'Maximilian, you can't kiss me when——'

'But I'm not kissing you—yet,' he added gruffly, his gaze holding hers hotly. '*Now* I'm kissing you.' His breath was warm against her mouth before his lips lowered to claim hers.

She didn't need him to tell her he was kissing her, she knew exactly what he was doing—for a fraction of a second, then she didn't know very much at all, except the feel, smell and taste of him. And he tasted so sweet, pure nectar, sipping from her lips now as if she were the flower that nurtured him, his tongue teasing an evocative path into the moist heat of her mouth, plundering, possessing, her body suddenly taut with a trembling need that began as a hot ache between her thighs, her nipples hard and thrusting beneath the thin material of her T-shirt.

The air was cool upon the nakedness of her skin as Maximilian pushed the T-shirt up out of his way, baring her breasts to his questing mouth, her gasp one of instinctive delight as he drew her nipple into the hot moisture of his mouth, his tongue loving the sensitised tip, each caress sending a new shuddering wave of pleasure through her already aroused body.

Her throat arched as he trailed kisses along the pulsing column of her throat, his hand gently cupping and caressing one bared breast now, the thumb-pad moving across a nipple still damp from the caress of his lips and tongue.

Sophie wanted to be close to him too, unbuttoning his shirt with hands that shook, fumbling slightly. Maximilian was growing impatient for the closeness himself, pulling at the shirt, ripping off two of the buttons in the process.

Sophie gave a shaky laugh as she looked down at the ruined shirt, the material actually torn where the buttons had come off. 'That's another shirt I owe you!'

Her hands trembled as she touched the hard dampness of his chest, the hair dark and silky there. To her delight his nipples reacted in a similar way to her own when she ran her fingertips over them. Malcolm had never been particularly interested in foreplay in their lovemaking, had certainly never encouraged Sophie to touch his body in the way Maximilian was now doing, guiding her hand to the hard need of his thighs. After initial wide-eyed surprise she gave in to the aching temptation to know all of his body in this way, loving the surge of pleasure she felt coursing through Maximilian as she slowly caressed him.

'I'll forget about the shirts,' he groaned raggedly, 'if you'll wear one of the pink ones to bed tonight. I've had the most erotic fantasies about you doing that ever since you first suggested it!'

In bed tonight... Did he mean——? She looked up at him with wide hazel eyes. 'Maximilian...?'

'If you don't stop saying that I'll have to make love to you right here and now!' he warned shakily, his eyes dark, an aroused flush to the hardness of his cheeks. 'And this is hardly the place!' he added self-derisively.

In a stable. Beside an expensive racehorse—Oh, God, yes, that damned racehorse! She had completely forgotten, as Maximilian made love to her, that it was because of the horse that Jennie was upstairs in her room in tears, that Sophie had come in search of Maximilian at all.

'Maximilian, what *is* Gracious Lady doing here?' She frowned up at him. 'Brian says she's a valuable race-horse. That she——'

She was thrust away from him so suddenly that she almost lost her balance completely and fell into the straw at their feet. And Maximilian was looking at her now with such cold suspicion that she hastily straightened her clothing to cover her nakedness, suddenly feeling very self-conscious, the desire that had been between them seconds ago disappearing completely.

'And just what the hell would he know about it?' he rasped harshly, eyes narrowed.

Sophie shrugged uncomfortably. 'He recognised the horse as a thoroughbred, and I suppose when he questioned Jennie about it she——'

'He had no damned right questioning my daughter about anything!' Maximilian bit out tautly. 'Who the hell is he, anyway? Besides the insensitive swine who left you to your fate on a dark road at midnight three days ago!'

So he *had* realised that, had he? Sophie hadn't thought it would take him long to add two and two together and come up with the appropriate answer!

She moistened her lips. 'I told you, he's a friend of mine who——'

'Some friend!' Maximilian scorned with feeling. 'Your choice of male friends could use a little more—discretion being applied,' he derided harshly.

He was being deliberately insulting now. 'You could be right...' She looked at him pointedly; after all, they had been on the brink of making love minutes ago. 'If you'll excuse me,' she told him stiffly, 'I think one of us should go and talk to Jennie!'

Maximilian didn't answer her gibe, had already turned away to talk soothingly to the racehorse.

Sophie stumbled in the straw as she went to move, but she wasn't sure whether that was because of the unevenness of the surface, or because her legs were still weak from Maximilian's kisses. Whichever, she was angry with herself for the lapse, slamming the stable door closed behind her as she left.

With any luck, the horse would be startled into trampling all over Maxim—— She came to an abrupt halt outside at the vengeful gruesomeness of her thoughts, listening intently for the sound of any snorting or stamping to show the spirited horse's temper. Nothing. Complete silence from inside the stable. No doubt Maximilian had the stupid horse eating out of his hand *too*; she certainly didn't seem to have any defence against him. He kissed her when he wanted to, and just pushed her away when he didn't!

She glared at Paul Wiseman on her way through the hallway as he stood there talking to one of the men who worked in the stables. Maximilian's assistant looked taken aback at the ferocity of her gaze, but at that moment Sophie was too angry to care what he thought was wrong with her. Everyone here seemed to be more concerned with the welfare of that stupid horse than they were with the people who lived here. It was only a horse, when all was said and done, whereas Jennie... Oh, damn Maximilian; she couldn't force him to show concern for his daughter if he didn't want to! Maybe Jennie was right after all—maybe he did care more for his horse than he did for her...

And Sophie couldn't love a man who cared more for his possessions than he did for his family; that would put Maximilian on a level with Malcolm, and she couldn't love anyone even remotely like him.

Although ... Wasn't it said that, no matter how your taste in a partner might seem to differ from one relationship to another, in actual fact, beneath the surface, those partners were probably very much alike; that she was more likely to go for a similar type to Malcolm, in fact, than any other...!

No, she couldn't believe that. Maximilian wasn't at all like Malcolm, and never could be!

Because she knew she *had* fallen in love with him...

It was ridiculous, totally illogical, utterly futile—despite the fact that Maximilian had admitted wanting and desiring her. Desire and wanting weren't the same as loving, and she wasn't about to settle for anything less than——

'Sophie, what are you doing mooning about in the hallway?' The sharply accusing voice of her aunt cut in on her tortuous thoughts.

And as she turned to face her aunt she realised she was indeed 'mooning about'; in fact, she was standing with one of her feet on the first stair, the other still in the carpeted hallway. Paul Wiseman, and the middle-aged man he had been talking to when she came in, seemed to have disappeared completely!

'Er—nothing,' she replied lamely, having stepped down completely into the hallway now.

Her aunt shook her head. 'Another meal ruined!' she dismissed impatiently. 'I've thrown more food away the last three days than I care to think about.'

Her aunt did look more than a little strained; in fact, she looked rather pale. 'Aunt Millie, are you feeling all right?' Sophie frowned.

'As a matter of fact, no,' her aunt muttered, guilty colour briefly entering her cheeks as she put a hand up to her temple. 'I must be getting old, Sophie,' she said wearily, pale once again, 'because all this upset seems to be bringing on one of my migraines!'

Oh, dear. Sophie remembered those migraines from childhood; her aunt didn't get them very often, possibly only once a year, but when she did it usually meant she had to take to her bed for twenty-four hours.

'Go to bed, Aunt Millie,' Sophie advised immediately. 'I can see to lunch——'

'I told you, no one wants any.' Her aunt shook her head, seeming to go paler by the second. 'It's dinner I'm more concerned with. May is only in until one o'clock, has already gone home, in fact, so she can't cook it. I was looking for Mr Grant to see if I could perhaps——'

'Don't worry any more, Aunt Millie. I'll find Maximilian and explain all this to him,' Sophie told her decisively, firmly turning her aunt back in the direction of her suite of rooms in the servants' quarters at the back of the house. 'And I'll see to dinner——'

'You?' Her aunt gave a pained frown as she came to an abrupt halt. 'But——'

'I can cook, Aunt Millie,' she assured her ruefully. 'And Jennie can help me,' she added firmly as the idea suddenly occurred to her; it would take care of two problems at the same time if she could get Jennie to come down to the kitchen to help her, keep the young girl occupied and in so doing give her less time to sit up in her room brooding. It would also get the meal cooked. Yes, it was a brilliant idea, even if she did say so herself. And between the two of them they were sure to be able to come up with something edible for dinner!

'Miss Jennie, help you cook dinner...?' Her aunt looked startled at the suggestion. 'But——'

'Will you just go, Aunt Millie?' she cajoled, sure that if her aunt didn't lie down soon she was going to have one of her really bad migraines, and that could incapacitate her for days rather than hours. Sophie was well aware that, although she might be able to produce something for them to eat for a couple of meals, after that things might start to flounder; her repertoire was a little limited!

It was evidence of just how bad her aunt felt, though, that she offered no further argument to the suggestion! 'You will explain to Mr Grant that I——?'

'Yes, of course I'll explain,' Sophie dismissed impatiently. Damn 'explaining to Mr Grant'; he would just have to put up with the inconvenience—and her cooking! It was time he learnt that not everyone could function like a machine, as he obviously did. 'Now just go.' She smiled reassuringly at her aunt as she personally took her to her bedroom and left her there.

Jennie still sat on her bed when Sophie entered the room after the briefest of knocks, a knock Jennie had chosen to ignore anyway. It was obvious from that almost vacuous look on Jennie's face that Maximilian still hadn't been up to see her.

'Come on, Jennie,' Sophie instructed briskly. 'Let's go downstairs; you and I have a meal to prepare for this evening,' she added as she received no response. Jennie turned to look at her now, frowning as she realised what Sophie had said.

'Yes.' Sophie grimaced in acknowledgement. 'I did say you and I are cooking dinner this evening. And if your cooking is anything like mine, we're going to need all the time between now and then to come up with something edible!'

To give Jennie her due, and despite the fact she was obviously still very upset over that scene with her father, once Sophie had explained the situation to her concerning Aunt Millie the girl threw herself into the idea of the two of them preparing dinner with a gusto Sophie could only applaud. And it soon became obvious, as Sophie became the helper and Jennie the cook, that Jennie had much more of an aptitude and liking for cooking than Sophie had ever had. In fact, Jennie had grudgingly confided, she was thinking of taking up some form of catering as a career once she had been to university.

They didn't have to worry about dessert at all, they discovered on checking the fridge for contents; the fresh fruit salad her aunt had made for lunch would do for that. But Jennie produced a wonderful prawn concoction as a starter, with a bought pâté as a standby for anyone who didn't like shellfish. And she soon had a chicken curry, made from the chicken that had been cooked for lunch and then not wanted, bubbling away in a pot on top of the cooker. It smelt absolutely marvellous, making Sophie glad she had thought of the idea of getting Jennie to help her in the first place!

Her own contribution to the proceedings was to make them both a sandwich and stave off the pangs of hunger until dinnertime!

As for telling Maximilian about her aunt, she couldn't even find him, let alone explain to him. Not that she looked too hard for him anyway, not all that anxious to see him again herself, still disgusted over his behaviour towards Jennie.

'He went out early this afternoon,' Jennie informed her dully as the two of them sat at the kitchen table drinking mugs of coffee and taking a well-earned break for a few minutes. 'You were wondering where my father was, weren't you?' she stated flatly as Sophie looked at her enquiringly. 'He went out in his car earlier. I heard him leave when I was shelling the prawns.' She shrugged dismissively. 'He's probably gone over to see Aunt Celia,' she announced with a grimace of distaste.

The fawning, pliant, eager-to-please Celia Taylor, who also didn't have any messy past to be coped with, any tangled present either.

'Don't look like that!' Jennie groaned as she watched the emotions flickering across Sophie's face. 'I'm his daughter, and, despite what other impression you may have got earlier, I love him. But for any woman to fall in love with him...!' She shook her head sadly.

Sophie gasped. 'But I don't——'

'You're starting to,' Jennie shrugged. 'If you haven't already...' She looked at Sophie closely, obviously not liking what she saw.

Sophie turned away from the intensity of that gaze, feeling totally exposed, her emotions laid bare. 'Jennie, your parents...?'

'Yes?' the young girl frowned darkly.

'What happened—between them?' She shook her head at the deeply personal question; she couldn't blame Jennie at all if she told her to mind her own damned business! She shouldn't be asking it of her really, knew that she shouldn't, but it was something she so needed to know. 'They don't sound as if—they were happy together?'

Jennie gave a disgusted snort at what she obviously thought was an understatement. 'They were in the process of getting a divorce when Mummy was killed in the car crash,' she revealed harshly. 'Who knows what went wrong between them?' She shrugged with a frown. 'All I knew was that it had become impossible to spend time with the two of them together. I was about nine when I first began to realise my parents weren't ecstatically happy together.' Her mouth twisted in self-derision. 'Actually, they weren't even mildly happy together. I suppose, like a lot of couples, they stayed together because of me. What happened to change that arrangement, I have no idea, but suddenly when I was twelve it was all-change and they decided to get divorced after all.' She shrugged. 'Maybe they had just decided by that time that I was old enough to accept that their marriage was over. I really don't know.' She shook her head.

When this young girl had been twelve, Sophie's own marriage had only just begun...

Now, almost four years later she had fallen in love with Jennie's father. And, as Jennie so rightly pointed out, that was pure madness!

'What's this?' Maximilian frowned as Jennie and Sophie brought in the prawn starters for the five of them to begin their meal, Paul Wiseman having joined them this evening. Sean was seated at the table with the other two men too.

Jennie glanced down at the prawn dish, somehow avoiding looking directly at her father, obviously still angry with him. 'You eat prawns, don't you?' she frowned.

'Of course I eat—— Where is Mrs Craine?' Maximilian watched with narrowed eyes as the two girls set the food on the table in front of him.

Sophie and Jennie had gone to great pains to make the table look as nice tonight as it did when Sophie's aunt did it, which was probably why the three men had had no idea, until they brought the food in, that it wasn't the housekeeper's work at all. But Sophie had no intention of letting her aunt down. Aunt Millie was fretting about her incapacity as it was, very anxious to attain assurances from Sophie as to the progress of dinner when Sophie had taken her in a cup of tea earlier. Sophie had been just as eager to get those same assurances as to whether or not Maximilian ate curry; it was such a specialised dish that, if he didn't, they were in trouble! Luckily, her aunt had assured her it was one of his favourite meals; Sophie wouldn't have put it past Jennie in her present state of mind to prepare something she knew her father hated!

Maximilian hadn't arrived back until just over an hour ago. Sophie had been in the kitchen still, giving the simmering curry a preoccupied stir, when she heard his car returning. As he passed the kitchen window, she could see he looked a lot less strained than he had earlier, and she couldn't help wondering if Celia Taylor had had something to do with that. No doubt the other woman had given him lunch as well.

At the thought of that, Sophie wondered why on earth she had gone to such trouble to make sure he wasn't inconvenienced over his dinner; it would have served him right if she had just left him to his own devices!

'Mrs Craine isn't feeling very well,' Jennie told her father as she took her own seat at the table beside Sean.

'I would have told you earlier—if I could have found you,' Sophie added sharply, sitting down abruptly too. She still hadn't told him about Brian's threats earlier yet—and even a woeful telephone call to Ally on her part hadn't been able to deter him from going ahead with his story; he was adamant that he was going to write it! But if Sophie couldn't even find Maximilian, then she couldn't tell him about that either, could she? So it was his own fault he didn't know about it. The time they had been together in Gracious Lady's stable didn't count!

'I had to go out,' he dismissed.

She met his gaze in steady challenge. 'I realised that.' And she had been tortured by thoughts of him and Celia together all afternoon. Oh, she had been kept busy, helping Jennie with the meal, but always at the back of her mind had been that nagging torment of what Maximilian and Celia were doing together all that time. 'So Jennie and I cooked the meal. Jennie mainly,' she added abruptly, no longer able to meet the coldness of Maximilian's gaze.

'And very nice it looks too,' Sean beamed at them appreciatively to make up for Maximilian's obvious lack of enthusiasm. 'You must have both worked very hard.'

'Oh, we did.' Jennie nodded, turning to Paul Wiseman, who sat at her other side. 'Come on, Paul, try a prawn,' she encouraged huskily, scooping a prawn up from his plate and holding it temptingly in front of him. 'Go on.' She smiled at him. 'They're delicious!'

Maximilian's mouth tightened, his eyes narrowed, as he watched the act of intimacy of his daughter feeding his employee the prawn.

Paul looked as if he would rather be anywhere else but sitting beside Jennie at that moment. Couldn't Maximilian see that Jennie was only behaving in the way she was to annoy him, that she had far from forgiven him for this morning?

Obviously not, Sophie realised with a sigh as his eyes seemed to glaze over coldly, his sense of humour sadly lacking where Jennie was concerned. His sense of proportion, too. Silly man, Sophie thought irritably, not having forgiven him for this morning herself yet either. But a smile curved her lips as she thought of how he would hate being thought 'silly'.

'Something amusing you, Sophie?' he rasped, cutting into her thoughts.

She gave him an almost guilty glance, realising even as she did so that he couldn't possibly know what she was thinking—he was clever, but not that clever; he actually believed her humour was at his expense concerning Jennie's antics with Paul.

'Not in the least,' she answered him coolly before turning to Jennie. 'This prawn dish is wonderful, Jennie,' she told her warmly, hoping to divert everyone's attention on to something less explosive than the tension between Maximilian and Jennie.

'Yes,' Maximilian agreed curtly, his mouth twisting wryly. 'Obviously your private education hasn't been a complete waste of time!'

Sophie winced at his deliberate barb; Maximilian was obviously furious.

Mealtimes were proving to be such a relaxing time in this household, Sophie thought heavily as she viciously stabbed a prawn up on to her own fork; she would be lucky if she didn't have an ulcer by the time she left!

When she left...

Oh, God, the thought of leaving Maximilian now, when she knew she had fallen in love with him, was like being told she was to have a limb amputated!

Only another six days and she would be out of his life—and his hair!—forever...

CHAPTER TEN

SOPHIE wasn't asleep when the intruder came stumbling into her bedroom. She had been lying awake in the darkness, wondering what she was going to do about her love for Maximilian, when the door suddenly burst open and someone almost fell into her bedroom.

She shot up into a sitting position in the bed, trying to focus in the darkness, her heart beating wildly in her breast at this intrusion. She had only moved into this bedroom next to Jennie's the day before, and as it was a guest bedroom it had been unoccupied before that, so she doubted that whoever it was had come in here by mistake; who was it?

The intruder stumbled again, groaning as he came into contact with the edge of the dressing-table placed near the door.

An incompetent burglar? He was surely making enough noise to have woken her even if she had originally been asleep!

She took a deep breath. 'Who is it?' she demanded, much more forcefully than she actually felt.

'I—oh, hell!' the man swore harshly as he stumbled over the stool that stood in from of the dressing-table now, landing on the carpeted floor with a heavy thump.

'Maximilian!' Sophie gasped as she instantly recognised his voice. 'I—what are you doing in here?' She was getting out of bed even as she spoke, crossing to his side, going down on her knees beside him on the floor as only a low groan answered her concerned query. 'Maximilian...?' she prompted in a puzzled voice,

148

reaching out to touch him, instantly withdrawing her hand as it came into contact with the bareness of his shoulder. It was difficult to see in the darkness, but— My God, was he completely naked...? If he were, that would explain *completely* what he was doing here!

Maximillian groaned beside her again, a low, obviously agonised sound that made Sophie forget everything but the fact that she had to help him. He had obviously hurt himself when he fell over the stool, might even have broken something. But because Sophie wasn't sure how he was dressed—or undressed, whichever the case might be!—she was loath to put the light on and actually look to see how he had injured himself.

'Maximillian, where does it hurt?' she prompted, reaching out to shake one bare shoulder when he didn't respond, hoping it wasn't his shoulder that hurt! 'Maximillian!' she urged again, growing impatient now.

God knew what would be thought of the two of them here together if anyone should go past her bedroom. Her only defence was that she hadn't invited him in here, had no idea why he was here—except the obvious reason, of course, and she couldn't use that as defence! All she knew was he had come stumbling into her bedroom like a—my God, he was *drunk*, Sophie realised incredulously. That had to be the answer, she realised as she sat back on her heels. He had been stumbling when he came into the bedroom, obviously hadn't been able to stand steadily on his own two feet even then.

'My stomach,' he suddenly moaned. 'Oh, God...!' He shuddered, his position on the floor almost foetal now.

He deserved to have a stomach ache if he had been drinking enough to make him like this, Sophie decided irritably. Couldn't he see he wasn't solving anything by getting—but neither was she, she realised self-derisively.

'Come on, Maximilian,' she instructed firmly, grasping his arm and attempting to pull him to his feet. It was an impossible task from the outset; he was a dead weight. Dead drunk! 'Maximilian!' she repeated sharply. 'At least help me to get you as far as the bed,' she sighed wearily. Although what she was actually going to do with him when she got him to the bed she had no idea; he couldn't stay here, drunk or not.

She found, to her relief, when she moved to switch on the bedside lamp, that he wasn't naked at all, although the brief black underwear he did have on was little enough covering, and very sexy! But it was better than nothing, and as she struggled to get him up on to the bed she tried not to look too intently at the bronzed litheness of his almost naked body. And as he seemed to have all the pliability of an octopus, seeming to have just as many limbs to control, this proved very difficult to do.

Sophie finally managed, after much heaving and tugging, to get him lying on top of her bed; unfortunately he was laying from side to side across the bed, with his feet dangling to the floor on one side! But he *was* on the bed. Unfortunately, so was she, one of her arms trapped beneath him where he had taken her with him!

'Maximilian!' she said again, more forcefully this time. She was sure, after tonight, that he wouldn't like the sound of his name on her lips at all; she sounded like a nagging fishwife!

His only answer was to roll over on one side—the wrong side, trapping her more firmly against him than ever!—throwing his arms about her waist and nuzzling his face into her throat.

Oh, God, Sophie thought dizzily. What was she supposed to do now? They couldn't stay here like this, her bedroom door still wide open, leaving them conspicuously obvious to anyone who should walk past her room in the morning, apparently locked in a passionate embrace! But neither, she discovered after trying for several minutes, could she free herself. And Maximilian was out cold!

Great. Just great! Here she was, held in the arms of the man she loved, wearing one of his pink shirts, as he had asked her to, and he was unconscious at her side. It was just too——

Suddenly he moved again, groaning, falling backwards on the duvet once more, his face twisted in agony. Agony? Surely that wasn't usual for someone who was just drunk? And—he didn't smell of drink!

Not at all, she discovered as she leant closer to him. He wasn't drunk at all!

Then what was wrong with him? She frowned down at him, noticing for the first time how pale his cheeks were beneath his tan, giving him an almost gray cast. But he had only bumped into the dressing-table and stool in front of it, he couldn't really have hurt himself that badly on them, and he had definitely been staggering when he came into the room.

He was ill! Oh, my God, the stomach pain wasn't being caused by drink at all. Appendicitis, then? It was a possibility, Sophie realised.

'Maximilian?' She moved up on to her knees beside him on the bed this time, leaning over him as she gently shook his shoulder. 'Darling, where does it hurt?' she prompted softly, not even aware at that moment that she had used the endearment, just so worried about him she couldn't think straight.

'Poisoned,' he managed to gasp. 'I've been—poisoned!'

She sat back, frowning down at him, completely stunned. What——? How——? 'Maximilian...?'

He was suddenly completely lucid as he looked up at her, his eyes dark with pain. 'Get me to the hospital, Sophie,' he told her through teeth gritted together in rigid control.

She blinked down at him. 'I'll call the doctor.' She began to scramble off the bed.

'There's no time for that.' Maximilian gasped as another wave of pain shot through him. 'Just drive me straight to the hospital. I need to get—whatever this is out of my system as quickly as possible. Please, Sophie,' he prompted savagely as she still hesitated about what to do.

She swallowed hard. 'Shall I get Sean?' She was pulling denims on over her panties even as she spoke, tucking the pink shirt hurriedly into the waistband. There was no time to change the latter, and no privacy either. Not that Maximilian was in any condition to notice what she was wearing!

'No, I don't want anyone else involved in this. Just you,' he told her as he struggled into a sitting position, still in obvious pain, although he looked down ruefully at his near-nakedness. 'But perhaps you should help me get some clothes on too before we go...?'

Sophie was surprised they didn't wake the whole household in their struggle to get Maximilian back to his bedroom and then into his clothes!

She felt hot and flustered by the time they had finally managed to get him into a shirt and trousers, kneeling down at his feet to lace his shoes.

'This isn't quite the way I had imagined having you at my feet!'

She looked up at him sharply at the huskily made statement, colour heating her cheeks at the burning intensity of his gaze as she straightened abruptly. 'You're obviously feeling a little better,' she bit out shortly, although in actual fact she knew she was being unfair to him; he looked absolutely dreadful, his face haggard, greyer than ever, a fine sheen of perspiration on his skin. It was the intimacy of the image his words had provoked that had shaken her into speaking so sharply. 'Maximilian, what makes you think you could have been——? We'd better go!' She rushed to his side as he was bent over double with the pain again. What did it matter at this moment why he thought he had been poisoned—although how, and by whom, she had no idea either? He was obviously in agony, and the sooner she got him to the hospital, the better.

She almost screamed her terror as, after she had eventually managed to get Maximilian down the stairs and out the front door, a shadow detached itself from the wall outside and a voice spoke in the darkness!

'Who's there?'

That was what she wanted to know; the stupid man had almost given her a heart attack!

'It's all right, Davies.' Maximilian was the one to answer him. 'Miss Gordon and I are just—going for a drive.'

A drive? Being taken to the hospital because he thought he had been poisoned could hardly be called that! But Maximilian was obviously in no mood to explain himself to Davies—whoever he was!—in any other way. Sophie was just too dazed and confused by the whole sequence of events to care any more...

'You can drive, I take it?' Maximilian handed her the keys to his car, getting into the passenger seat without waiting for her reply.

Yes, she could drive, but she rarely did so, because she couldn't afford a car of her own, and she had never driven anything as powerful as Maximilian's luxurious BMW. Malcolm had certainly never let her anywhere near his precious Porsche!

She was more than a little nervous about driving the BMW at all, but when Maximilian lapsed into semi-consciousness again almost as soon as they had driven down the driveway her nervousness dissipated and she just concentrated on finding her way to the hospital.

Considering, she thought ruefully as she drove, what a restrained and controlled man Maximilian was—except in stables, and when he imagined her going to bed in one of his shirts!—her life had certainly been very eventful since she met him. And to think she had imagined this would just be another dull week of the work she needed to do to fund her studies; there was nothing 'dull' about being near Maximilian!

'For goodness' sake, Jennie, just calm down,' Sophie attempted to soothe with a frown, watching the young girl as she sprang to her feet and began pacing the room in agitated movements. 'I told you, your father is fine now,' she dismissed. 'And——'

'But it's my fault,' Jennie choked, looking far younger than her sixteen years at the moment.

Sophie had returned to the house a short time ago after spending most of what was left of the night at the hospital with Maximilian. He had been right about the poisoning, had received treatment for it at the hospital, was even now sleeping it off in a hospital bed, the danger passed.

Sophie had gone straight to the kitchen on her return, only to find her aunt already up and about, apparently fully recovered, if a little pale, breakfast already set out in the morning-room. She had avoided her aunt's searching looks, going off in search of toast and coffee— what passed for the latter out of the machine at the hospital certainly couldn't be identified as such!—only to find Jennie already seated at the table having her own breakfast.

She had known, for all their arguments, that Jennie was going to be upset about her father, but the worst was over now, and Sophie was sure Maximilian wasn't about to start pointing fingers.

'It was no one's fault, Jennie,' she dismissed, sipping her coffee. 'There was no way of knowing——'

'*I* knew,' Jennie wailed, her face contorted with guilt. 'But I only wanted him to get a little stomach ache, because he's been so mean to me, and——'

'Jennie, no one could have foreseen that one of those prawns was—what do you mean?' She frowned at the young girl as she realised what she had said. 'Jennie, what are you talking about?' She shook her head dazedly.

The young girl swallowed hard, chewing on her bottom lip. 'I know Daddy can't eat garlic, that it disagrees with him, and so I——'

'Garlic?' Sophie repeated dismissively. 'But I told you, Jennie, it was one of the prawns that gave your father a serious case of food poisoning.' And Maximilian had been very ill indeed by the time they arrived at the hospital; in fact he had been almost delirious.

'It was the garlic,' Jennie insisted stubbornly. 'I put a little in the curry, knowing all the other spices and flavours would disguise it.' She winced at the memory.

Sophie frowned at her. 'You wanted to make your father ill...?' Only that fact seemed important at the moment. 'You deliberately gave him something you knew would make him sick?' She couldn't believe Jennie was capable of doing such a thing, to her father, of all people. Or was he the *one* person...?

The young girl began to cry now. 'Garlic usually gives him heartburn, that's all, keeps him awake all night.' She sniffed inelegantly. 'It's never made him this ill before.'

And it hadn't made him this ill this time either. The doctor at the hospital had been absolutely certain that was a prawn. Although Maximilian's having eaten the garlic that disagreed with him couldn't have helped the situation! Poor Maximilian.

'Jennie——' Sophie moistened her lips, trying to think what to say; what Jennie had done had far more serious implications than merely trying to give her father a bad night's sleep. 'The garlic aside, it *was* a prawn that made your father so ill last night.'

Jennie blinked at her uncertainly, paling even more as she saw the truth of Sophie's words in her steady hazel-coloured gaze, and dropping down heavily into her chair. 'I thought—I believed—— Oh, Sophie!' she cried, burying her face in her hands.

Sophie went to her unhesitatingly, putting her arms about her, hugging her tightly. What Jennie had done had been spiteful and childish, but it hadn't been dangerous. At the same time, it was evidence of just how badly the relationship between Maximilian and his daughter had deteriorated. And that certainly wasn't because the two didn't care for each other. Sophie had seen how much Jennie loved her father, and she had witnessed—and personally felt!—Maximilian's distress yesterday when he'd thought Jennie had disappeared. Communication had, for some reason, broken down between the two of them, and Sophie was sure it had something to do with the accusations Jennie had levelled at her father yesterday. And the situation couldn't go on. Before, they had just been hurting each other emotionally; now, with Jennie's confession, it had progressed beyond that.

'What am I going to do?' Jennie clung to Sophie in childish need.

'We are going to the hospital to talk to your father,' Sophie told her firmly.

'I couldn't,' the young girl shook her head protestingly. 'He's going to hate me when he realises what I've done!'

'Don't be silly, Jennie,' Sophie dismissed gently. 'Your father could never hate you.'

'No?' Jennie grimaced doubtfully. 'How would you feel towards me if you knew I had deliberately spiked your food with something I knew disagreed with you?'

Hopping mad, was Sophie's immediate inward response. As she had no doubt Maximilian would too. But at the same time, this was hardly something she could keep to herself. Not that she thought Jennie would ever be silly enough to do something like this again; the whole incident had obviously frightened the young girl very badly.

'Perhaps, in a few moments,' rasped a harshly authoritative voice from behind them both, 'you would care to explain that remark! But right now I have something more important I want to talk to Sophie about.'

Maximilian!

Sophie gasped in surprise when she turned and saw him standing there; the last time she had seen him he had been stretched out in a hospital bed, very pale against the bedclothes, having lapsed into an exhausted sleep after being violently ill.

He still looked very pale, grey almost, and there was a dampness to his skin revealing the obvious effort it was taking to be on his feet at all.

'Maximilian, what are you doing here?' Sophie hurriedly crossed the room to his side. 'You shouldn't be out of bed,' she added worriedly; what were the doctors thinking of, letting him leave hospital so quickly?

He looked at her now with such contempt that she was halted in her tracks before she even reached him, gazing up at him uncertainly. What had happened since she'd left him a couple of hours ago, grateful to her for helping him in the way she had, to turn him into this cold, forbidding stranger who looked as if he would like to choke the life out of her with his bare hands? She realised, from his initial remark, that he must have overheard at least part of her conversation with Jennie, and so know some of what had gone on last night; but that should have directed his anger at Jennie, not at her.

'I had no choice,' he bit out coldly, his gaze never leaving her face.

She shook her head dazedly. 'But the doctors at the hospital wouldn't have let you——'

'I didn't ask them,' he scorned hardily.

Her eyes widened. 'You mean——'

'I discharged myself,' he grated. 'As I said, I had no choice.'

Sophie didn't even begin to understand what he was talking about; what she did know was that he shouldn't be out of bed. If he didn't soon sit down he was going to fall down!

'I had no choice,' he repeated for the third time, 'once I had seen this!'

'This' was a newspaper, which he threw down on the table with obvious disgust.

A newspaper...

And Sophie suddenly knew, without even looking at it, that Brian had gone ahead with his threat and written his story!

CHAPTER ELEVEN

'LEAVE us, Jennifer,' Maximilian instructed his daughter abruptly.

'But——'

'After what I overheard a few minutes ago,' he continued in a hard voice, 'I don't think you're in any position to argue—do you?'

Jennie's lips clamped together in defeat, biting back any further protest. But she was far from cowed, either by what had happened last night or her father's harshness now, despite the fact that she had been so upset a few minutes ago; Maximilian's return, obviously with no serious ill-effects except that paleness to his skin, seemed to have restored Jennie's defiance. Although she moved obediently to the door now. Probably just glad to be escaping so lightly, Sophie decided!

'But don't disappear completely,' Maximilian warned softly before the young girl could leave the room. 'We still have *such* a lot to talk about!'

Guilty colour darkened Jennie's cheeks as she hurriedly left the room, closing the door on her escape with obvious relief.

Sophie had made use of their brief exchange to pick up the newspaper Maximilian had thrown down so disgustedly minutes earlier. She didn't have far to look for the article that had so incensed him; he had left the newspaper open on the appropriate page! Sophie didn't even get as far as reading the article itself, highlighted with a photograph of Maximilian and Jennie standing together at a race meeting, a smaller one of Sophie beneath this—Brian had obviously found one of her childhood photographs that Ally had, and used that; she must have been all of sixteen herself when it was taken! The headline with the story read, 'Lady Sophie, "family companion"', the implication obvious; and with that ridiculously old photograph of her to accompany it it gave the impression of Maximilian's being a cradle-snatcher, if nothing else! No wonder he was incensed!

The first paragraph only confirmed her worst imaginings.

Lady Sophie Gordon, divorced daughter of the impoverished Earl and Countess Gordon, was employed by the Grant family as companion to the heir to the Grant fortune, sixteen-year-old daughter Jennifer, but it would seem Maximilian Grant and Lady Sophie are the ones having 'fun' together'!

Tears clouded her vision at the insulting tone of the article, and she found she couldn't see to read any more. Not that she wanted to. People didn't actually read this awful rubbish and believe it, did they? she inwardly wailed. Brian, how could you? she choked inside!

'Tacky doesn't even begin to describe that particular publication,' Maximilian rasped with obvious disgust. 'I won't even classify it as a newspaper, because it doesn't even attempt to print news, only gossip—erroneous gossip at that!' he added hardly.

Sophie blinked rapidly, forcing herself to read the rest of the article. It was nothing short of libellous—although it cleverly did just fall short of that! It implied that her role as companion to Jennifer had just been a smoke-screen from the first, that Sophie was in fact Maximilian's latest mistress. Brian couldn't be ambitious enough to write lies like this—could he...?

'One of the young nurses at the hospital saw the photographs, recognised me as the new patient, and thought I would love to see myself in print!' Maximilian told her grimly. 'Naturally I telephoned the owner of the newspaper as soon as I had read the damned thing,' he continued remorselessly, his gaze cold on Sophie. 'He told me that they had attained their information from a "reliable friend of the family",' he bit out tautly. '*Your* family, I believe!'

She swallowed hard, feeling ill at the details of her private life the newspaper had padded the story out with—her poor but titled parents, her disastrous marriage to Malcolm. The implication seemed to be that, because of her family's straitened circumstances, Lady Sophie maintained her life in society by the support of her rich lovers. Rich lovers! My God, there had been no one in her life since Malcolm, and he had been her husband, not her lover, and he certainly hadn't been rich. But the implication was there, none the less.

'Oh, Brian...' she groaned weakly.

'Burnett, yes,' Maximilian confirmed knowingly, his gaze glacial. 'Or were you in this together?' His eyes were narrowed.

Sophie's head snapped back as if she had been struck. 'What...?'

'What a damn fool I've been!' Maximilian shook his head in self-disgust as this idea took root and grew—out of all proportion as far as Sophie was concerned! He thrust his hands into his trouser-pockets—as if the dangerous impulse to choke the life out of her hadn't completely passed. 'I was actually starting to—I believed you were what you seemed to be,' he scorned self-derisively. 'I even felt sorry for you, which was why I——'

'I don't need your pity!' Sophie snapped out of the stunned disbelief that had held her in its thrall since reading that newspaper. Who did this man think he was? Just whose reputation did he think had been ripped to shreds by that stupid newspaper, anyway? He had come out of this just looking like a rich man using a young woman until he tired of her, whereas she—— But, of course, Maximillian didn't think she had a reputation to lose. The arrogant——! 'I am exactly what I seem to be, Mr Grant.' She threw the newspaper down, angry colour blazing in her cheeks, freckles standing out lividly, her eyes a deep sparkling green. 'It's all a question of what you perceive!' Her whole body was tense with anger. 'You may have been hurt in the past—I really have no idea why you're so cynical and judgemental—but what I do know is, you're far from the first person to be hurt—or disillusioned. My husband married me for my title, and made no secret of that fact once we were safely married. He gambled away what little money we did have, and turned violent when I tried to stop him. But I don't hate or distrust *all* men because of what Malcolm did to me——'

'I don't hate and distrust all women either!' Maximilian defended scathingly.

'No?' Sophie gave him a pitying look. 'You certainly don't like any of us very much, not even your own daughter——'

'Leave Jennifer out of this——'

'Jennie,' Sophie cut in firmly. 'She prefers to be called Jennie, but you don't even seem to care!'

His mouth was a thin, angry line at the rebuke. 'I don't give a damn what she "prefers" to be called; her name is Jennifer!'

'No, I can see that you don't care,' Sophie scorned, shaking her head. 'But I wouldn't worry about that too

much, if I were you—if you do!—because it really isn't
going to matter for too much longer.'

His eyes were narrowed to icy slits now. 'What the
hell is that supposed to mean?'

'Work it out for yourself, Mr Grant; you seem to think
you know all the answers!' Sophie was breathing hard
in her agitation, pushed beyond all reasonable limita-
tions; Maximilian had insulted not only her motives but
her integrity.

He glared at her. 'Jennifer's actions are none of your
business.'

'She deliberately gave you garlic at dinner last night
because she knows it makes you ill!' Sophie told him
exasperatedly. 'That amounts to much more than a
childish prank. Either you have to talk to Jennie about
what she's doing, or someone else does——'

'None of *this*,' he cut in impatiently, indicating the
newspaper, 'has anything to do with Jennifer. And *she*
is no longer any of your concern, either,' he added
hardly.

No, Sophie had already gathered that much. Not that
she would have wanted to stay on here now. Far too
much had been said for her to be able to remain anywhere near Maximilian. But whether she went or stayed
made no difference to the fact that the situation between
Jennifer and her father was taking on much more serious
implications than was safe, for either of them.

'She is yours, though,' Sophie tried once more to
reason with Maximilian, in more controlled tones this
time; losing their tempers with each other wasn't
achieving anything. 'Believe what you like about me.'
She shrugged. 'Every other woman, if you want to. But
don't shut Jennie out. She loves you very much.'

'I told you——' he looked at her with cold disdain
'—my daughter is none of your concern.'

Sophie's anger was fading now, and in its place was a deep sadness. Was Maximilian's judgement so warped by his blindness towards Jennie that he couldn't even see what he was destroying? Obviously it was. And he was pushing *her* away too—because he had sensed that she too was coming to love him? Possibly. Although, from what he had said, his own responses to her had been because he 'felt sorry for her'! Which was the last thing she wanted from him. Even his contempt was preferable to his pity!

'Take another look at that newspaper, Maximilian,' she advised scornfully. 'And think who really comes off the worst in it! My God, Brian may have been stupid and hurtful, but you're being even more so.'

Maximilian continued to look at her coldly. 'Thankfully, your opinion means little or nothing to me,' he dismissed scathingly.

He deliberately meant to wound—and he succeeded; more, perhaps, than even he could know. 'But apparently your horse Gracious Lady is *very* important to you,' she said dully. 'And that's the story Brian *didn't* write.'

Maximilian's head snapped back suspiciously. 'What do you mean?'

She shrugged, having nothing else to lose now; she was definitely leaving here this time. 'I've already told you that he knows Gracious Lady is a racehorse.'

'So?' Maximilian bit out abruptly, eyes narrowed.

Sophie sighed at this stubbornness in refusing to see what she was trying to say. 'So what is a racehorse doing here?' she said wearily.

'None of your damned——'

'*I'm* not the one who cares, Maximilian!' she cut in exasperatedly. 'Are you so wrapped up in your own sense of indignation, over a newspaper story we both know is absolute rubbish, that you can't even see what I'm trying to point out to you?' She glared at him. '*I* don't care whether you have a string of racehorses actually living in your house with you, if that's what you want, but Brian was deeply intrigued by the fact that you have Lady here——'

'Then he can stop being "intrigued",' Maximilian's mouth twisted scornfully. 'Because she isn't here any more!'

'Not—But...?' She looked at him dazedly.

The horse had been here yesterday—hadn't it? Of course it had, she rebuked herself, it had been in the horse's stall that she and Maximilian had almost—— Where was the horse now? When had she been taken away? How? What on earth was going on?

She realised she was getting as bad as Brian for nosing into things that didn't concern her, but at the same time the horse's sudden disappearance was very curious.

'Sophie?' Maximilian returned mockingly, his gaze challenging.

Her cheeks became flushed at his taunt. 'I'll go and get my things together——'

'I'm surprised you managed to unpack them from the last time!' he derided harshly.

'Yes,' she accepted dully. 'My time here does seem to have been—eventful.'

'Eventful!' he echoed with disgust. 'I should never have let Jennifer talk me round into letting the two of you stay on here in the first place! If I hadn't I wouldn't have——' He broke off abruptly, his mouth a thin line. 'Was it all an act, Sophie?' He frowned. 'Did you and your boyfriend just want a story?'

'He isn't my boyfriend!' she defended heatedly. 'And I told you, he didn't even write the real story——' It was her turn to break off abruptly this time as a knock sounded on the door, immediately followed by Sean's entrance.

The older man looked at them with narrowed, questioning eyes, Maximilian pale and accusing, Sophie equally pale as she felt sick with reaction.

A dark frown settled over Sean's brow. 'There's a telephone call for you, Sophie,' he told her. 'I wouldn't have disturbed the two of you,' he added with a challenging look in Maximilian's direction as the younger man opened his mouth to issue a cutting remark at being interrupted in this way just because Sophie had a telephone call. 'But the young man was most insistent that he had to speak to you now.'

Young man...? Brian. It had to be. As she had intended talking to him herself once she left here, his call had saved her the bother of tracking him down. Her mouth tightened as she thought of exactly what she wanted to say to him.

'Your boyfriend obviously telephoning to warn you,' Maximilian drawled scornfully as he too realised who her caller was. 'He's a little late!'

'Warn her about what?' Sean frowned. 'Max, Davies reported to me that you left the house with Sophie at two o'clock this morning.' He looked questioningly at his friend and employer. 'Does that have anything to do with your conversation with Sophie now?'

Maximilian's mouth had tightened at the mention of last night. 'Only indirectly,' he grated. 'I should go and take your telephone call, Sophie,' he drawled with hard derision, his gaze coldly dismissive. 'And warn him the Lady story is definitely not for printing,' he added harshly as Sophie reached the door.

She glanced back at him, his face hard and uncompromising. She had no doubt he would turn Brian's ambitions into dust if the other man should dare to write that particular story! She felt a shiver of apprehension down her own spine at the icy threat emanating from Maximilian. She, she knew he was saying, would do well to heed the warning as much as Brian.

But she didn't *know* what the mystery was surrounding Lady's presence here. Didn't want to know it either!

'I'll tell him,' she nodded dully. 'Goodbye, Sean,' she added huskily, having come to like the older man even in the short time she had known him.

'Goodbye?' he repeated dazedly. 'But I thought——'

'Leave it, Sean,' Maximilian rasped harshly, giving the other man a silencing frown.

'But, Max——'

'I said leave it!' he bit out between gritted teeth.

'You can take the call in the study, Sophie,' Sean told her vaguely, still obviously completely puzzled by what was going on.

She looked at Maximilian's unyielding face, at the coldness in his eyes for her, and gave a choked cry before running to the door and leaving the room. She loved Maximilian, and he hated her. Oh, God . . . !

She was shaking very badly by the time she reached the study, and it took her several minutes to calm down enough to be able to pick up the telephone receiver and talk to Brian.

But he was in such a panic himself, over what had been printed in the newspaper, that he didn't seem to notice Sophie's emotional state, desperate for her to realise the story the newspaper had printed this morning was not the one he had given them, that he had given them something else completely.

'All that garbage about you and Grant,' he added disgustedly. 'I couldn't believe it when I opened the newspaper this morning and saw what they had printed about the two of you.'

'Let's hope no one else believes it either,' Sophie told him flatly, filled with utter despair at having to part from Maximillian in this way.

'Grant is going to be so—— Maybe he won't see it?' Brian suggested hopefully.

'He's already seen it,' Sophie told him drily.

For a moment Brian seemed thunderstruck by this, then, 'And?' he prompted in a hushed voice, obviously dreading her answer.

'He's going to have it framed and put on his bedroom wall—how do you *think* he feels about it, Brian?' she said exasperatedly.

'Er—angry?'

'Furious,' she confirmed unsympathetically. 'Murderously so,' she added shakily, sure that, if Sean hadn't interrupted them in the way that he had, Maximilian might just have given in to the temptation he had been fighting for so long, and actually strangled her!

'Oh, God!' Brian groaned. 'I'll come and see him, try to explain——'

'I wouldn't,' Sophie warned. 'Not unless you want to be his first victim!'

'But——'

'Just leave it, Brian.' She sighed wearily. 'And steer your ambition in some other direction than the Grant family,' she added firmly. 'I have to go now, Brian,' she added hastily as he would have protested again. 'I'll give you a ring in a few days.' She rang off quickly, before he could object further, or probe too deeply into Maximilian's reaction to the newspaper; if he were to realise Maximilian had ordered her from the house because of it, because of what he suspected was her part in attaining the story, she didn't doubt that Brian would insist on coming out here himself to explain things to Maximilian. She knew, better than anyone, it seemed, that it would achieve nothing, and that it would only delay her departure. And she very badly needed to get away from here now.

Jennie's bedroom door stood open as Sophie passed on the way to her room further down the corridor, a half-packed suitcase open on the bed...

Sophie stopped in the doorway, watching Jennie as she moved about the room putting more things inside the case. 'Going somewhere?' she finally prompted lightly.

Jennie spun round guiltily, her relief immense at seeing it was only Sophie who stood there. 'Back to school.' She shrugged dismissively. 'Some of the other girls were staying on during the holiday anyway, and I think it might be safer if I go and join them.' She gave a pointed grimace.

'Jennie, it really was a prawn that made your father so ill,' she gently reassured the young girl.

'But don't you see? The intent was there!' Jennie groaned self-disgustedly. 'I wanted to make him sick because he was being so mean to me all the time.'

'But it wasn't you who——'

'It doesn't matter, can't you see?' Jennie looked at her pleadingly, her eyes filled with tears. 'I love my father, Sophie, and I——'

'I'm very glad to hear it.' Maximilian spoke softly from just behind Sophie, causing her to turn and face him with a startled gasp. 'Because I happen to love you too—Jennie,' he added gruffly.

Jennie just stared at him, dumbstruck by his admission—and his use of the diminutive of her name that she preferred and which he had steadfastly refused to use.

Sophie looked at him too, but warily. His manner towards Jennie seemed to have softened, but that was no reason to suppose she was included in this sudden gentleness. In fact, she had every reason to believe he never wanted to see her again!

As he entered the bedroom fully Maximilian's gaze narrowed on the half-packed suitcase that lay on the bed. 'What's this?' He frowned at his daughter.

She flushed uncomfortably. 'I thought it might be better, for everyone,' she added breathlessly, 'if I just went back to school.'

Maximillian pulled a face. 'For me, you mean.' He shook his head. 'My God, Sean was right, I've made a complete mess of this whole business! You've decided to go back to school, Sophie is leaving——'

'What!' Jennie gasped, looking at Sophie questioningly.

'—and so is Sean,' Maximilian continued, as if Jennie hadn't made the interruption.

'Sean is . . . ?' Jennie was obvious stunned. 'But—but he's been with you for years! Why on earth would he want to leave?' She frowned.

Maximilian grimaced. 'Because of you.'

'Me?' Jennie echoed, looking more puzzled than ever.

Sophie could guess exactly why Sean had told Maximilian he was leaving; the older man was obviously very fond of Jennie, considered her part of his family, and he deplored the way Maximilian treated her as much as Sophie did! Had someone finally got through to Maximilian—had Sean's decision to leave actually shocked him into seeing sense? She certainly hoped so!

'Jennie.' Maximilian looked at his daughter with eyes softened to a grey-blue. 'I—there have been complications during this school holiday that——'

'So I'm a "complication" now, am I?' the over-sensitive Jennie pounced heatedly. 'That's just another name for a nuisance. Well, you needn't worry any longer, because I'm going!' She threw some clothes into the suitcase.

'Jennie——'

'And you needn't worry that you'll be alone once Sophie, Sean and I have gone,' she scornfully cut across her father's gently reasoning tone, looking out of the window on to the driveway now. 'Because Aunt Celia has arrived to keep you company!' She looked across the room at Maximilian with defiant challenge.

'Celia . . . !' Maximilian groaned impatiently, obviously not in the least pleased at the prospect as he crossed to Jennie's side at the window. 'Just what I need,' he muttered after looking down on to the driveway himself, turning back with irritated movements to look at Sophie. 'Could you possibly go downstairs and talk to Celia while I——?'

'Me?' It was Sophie's turn to gasp now.

Why on earth would she want to go down and talk to Celia Taylor? More to the point, after Celia's rather pointed aversion to her company the last time the two of them had met, why should they—any of them— assume Celia would want to talk to her?

'If you would?' Maximilian looked at her pleadingly. 'I need to talk to Jennie.'

Sophie looked at him searchingly, realising, as she did so, what it was costing him to ask for her help in this way at all. And he *was* asking for her help, desperately needed to resolve his differences with Jennie—because he now knew, as she had warned him would happen, that he was close to losing his daughter forever if he didn't soon do something.

Sophie knew that, no matter what her own relationship with Maximilian, she wasn't proof against such a plea...

CHAPTER TWELVE

'*LADY* SOPHIE GORDON?' Celia drawled, the folded newspaper she held beating a steady tattoo against her trouser-clad thigh, her eyes narrowed in new critical assessment as she looked Sophie up and down.

Without quite knowing how it had happened, Sophie had found herself going down to the sitting-room, where her aunt had shown Maximilian's visitor, a few minutes ago. But Celia wasn't sitting, and from her restlessly agitated movements about the room, she had no intention of doing so!

'That's right,' Sophie acknowledged the accusation with a dismissive shrug. 'Would you like me to get you some coffee while you're waiting?' she offered uncomfortably.

What on earth was she doing, attempting to entertain Celia Taylor, of all people, when a short time ago Maximilian had ordered her out of his home?

She was doing it, she knew, because upstairs in Jennie's bedroom just now he had asked her to do it so nicely she hadn't the heart to refuse him!

Celia's top lip curled back scornfully. 'And you're *Max's* companion, not Jennifer's at all!'

Sophie frowned at that statement. If Celia had a relationship with Maximilian, why would the other woman believe such an outrageous claim by that not very reputable newspaper?

Because they *didn't* have a relationship, Sophie suddenly realised, no matter how deeply the other woman might wish it were otherwise.

173

Celia still tapped the newspaper against her thigh. 'No wonder he decided, in spite of the threats, to keep the two of you here with him rather than coming to my house. And I thought it was because he was being protective of me!' she added self-derisively. 'What a stupid fool I've been all these years!' She shook her head.

Threats? What threats?

Obviously Celia thought—because she believed that ridiculous claim in the newspapers about a relationship between Maximilian and Sophie!—that Maximilian would have told her what Celia was now talking about.

And suddenly, like a glimmer of light at the end of a very dark tunnel, it was all starting to make sense...

There was Maximilian's suspicion of her when he had first met her in the kitchen and hadn't realised who she was. There was that sudden decision of his not to have Jennie here after all. There was a new assistant, Paul Wiseman, whom Jennie had never even heard of. There were all those other 'new' members of staff Maximilian had told them about. There was that order about not leaving the house to go anywhere without telling someone where they were going. There were any number of incidents which, now she thought about them, had either seemed odd or heartless at the time, which could all make sense if—— There was Gracious Lady's presence here!

'I think perhaps you should discuss that with Maximilian,' she told the other woman noncommittally now; there was a lot she now wanted to discuss with Maximilian herself!

'What would be the point?' Celia dismissed impatiently, throwing the newspaper down disgustedly. 'It was a mistake for me to come here at all. Tell Max——'

'Tell Max what?' he queried curiously as he entered the room and almost walked into Celia on the point of leaving it. 'Steady!' He grasped her arm to stop her from losing her balance, frowning down at her flushed face. 'Celia . . . ?'

The beautiful woman shook off his restricting hands, her eyes flashing deeply violet. 'What a lot of years I've wasted waiting for you to notice me!' she snorted self-derisively. 'But my God, no more!' She tossed the dark thickness of her hair back over her shoulder. 'You're living in false hopes, Lady Sophie,' she turned and said challengingly to Sophie as she stood across the room, quietly witnessing the exchange, 'if you think you've found a permanent place in his life.' Her mouth twisted. 'So enjoy it while you can!' she advised mockingly. 'Goodbye, Max!' She stormed out of the room, her departure from the house heard seconds later as the front door closed with a loud slam.

Complete silence followed this heated departure, and Sophie was almost afraid to look at Maximilian; he was sure to think, having the opinion of her that he now did, that she had said or done something to bring about that explosion from Celia, was never going to believe her even if she claimed otherwise. Well, it was his own fault; he must have known Celia didn't like her!

She risked a tentative peep up at him between lowered lashes, her lids flying wide open as she saw he was grinning. Not just grinning, actually, but smiling from ear to ear, it seemed! 'Maximilian . . . ?' she said with slow uncertainty. Minutes ago he had been breathing fire and brimstone, and she couldn't think of anything that could have happened in the intervening minutes to change that. And yet he was definitely smiling . . .

'There you go again,' he murmured huskily. 'You know what hearing you say my name does to me!'

Sophie was totally stunned as he took her in his arms and kissed her!

In fact, for several seconds she was so stunned that she didn't move—and then she remembered all too clearly how Maximilian had ordered her to leave earlier!

'Stop that!' She pushed away from him, her face flushed. 'What do you think you're doing?'

'Kissing you,' he shrugged. 'And I think I must be doing it wrong, because there seems to be some confusion as to what I'm doing every time I *do* kiss you!'

'I know you were kissing me,' Sophie snapped frustratedly. 'I meant——'

'Every time I kiss the woman I love,' he added thoughtfully.

'What do—you—think...?' She trailed off lamely, looking at him with widely disbelieving eyes; he couldn't have been talking about her? But who else was there in the room!

'The woman my daughter assures me loves me in return,' Maximilian murmured as he put his arms about her again. 'Although she also said that I, quote, "don't deserve you", unquote.' He looked down at her with tenderly loving eyes. 'I don't think I do either, but, if you're agreeable, I would like to keep you.'

Sophie opened her mouth to speak, and when no words came out she closed it again, opening her mouth a second time, and as quickly closing it again. She knew she must look like a fish out of water, but for the moment she couldn't seem to do anything else!

'Keep me?' she finally managed to choke out, latching on to the part of the statement she could deal with. 'Don't start believing your own publicity, Maximilian——'

'I wasn't talking about that sort of "keeping you",' he rasped impatiently. 'I meant, I would like you to stay in my life. As my wife,' he added huskily.

Sophie couldn't breathe, coughing and spluttering, choking for breath, sure she must have misheard him; Maximilian couldn't *really* have asked her to marry him!

'I know I've been unreasonable and pig-headed with you—Jennie's choice of words, not mine,' he explained with a grimace. 'I happen to believe I've just been a straightforward bastard to you.' He groaned self-disgustedly. 'I know it's not really an acceptable excuse, but this last week has been one of the most worrying I've ever known.' He frowned.

'Because of the threats against Lady.' Sophie nodded understandingly, slowly recovering from the shock he had given her, especially now they were talking about something she *could* answer. 'And Jennie,' she added softly.

Maximilian's frown deepened. 'How did you know about them?'

'Don't start that again!' she warned impatiently, moving away from him completely. 'Celia told me just now. She was so upset about the story in the newspaper about the two of us that I don't think she particularly cared what she said any more!' Sophie shook her head ruefully. 'I'm not really surprised. It was the biggest load of—God, it was awful!' She shuddered to think what her parents—and Aunt Millie!—were going to have to say about it.

Maximilian nodded grimly. 'What did Burnett have to say for himself?'

Sophie shook her head. 'He's as upset about it as we are—well, probably not quite as much as we are,' she grimaced, 'because he isn't personally mentioned in the article, but——'

'You're burbling again, woman,' Maximilian told her indulgently.

'Well, of course I'm burbling!' She looked up at him exasperatedly. 'You and Jennie are at odds with each other——'

'Not any more,' Maximilian assured her confidently. 'Oh, I have no doubts we will have our ups and down in future, like any parent and child—in fact, I'm sure we will!' he acknowledged ruefully. 'We're too much alike for it to be any other way. Yes, I do realise that.' He looked at Sophie with raised brows as she smiled knowingly. 'But at least now Jennie realises that I've been the way I have because I love her, not because I don't want her in my life. Now, why else are you burbling, Sophie?' He looked at her mockingly now.

Sophie gave him a feigned glare, absolutely delighted that he seemed to have sorted things out between himself and Jennie. And he was right, it would still be far from easy between father and daughter the next few years, possibly until Jennie was out of her teens. But as long as Jennie knew Maximilian loved her, it should never be this bad between them ever again.

'Then there are those threats,' Sophie reminded worriedly.

'There *were* those threats,' Maximilian told her firmly. 'I had received several telephone calls telling me to withdraw Lady from a certain race, that if I didn't something would happen to either the horse or Jennie. It isn't so unusual for owners to receive threats like that, and usually they turn out to be a hoax. But this one had much more serious undertones, especially when Lady became mysteriously ill several days ago and it didn't look as if she was going to be able to race anyway. The next telephone call after that claimed that Jennie could be next, and that she might not get off as lightly as Lady. I brought the horse here where I could keep a closer eye on her, decided it would be better for Jennie to go to

Celia—with suitable security, of course,' he added grimly. 'But it's no longer necessary; the young stablehand who was being paid to nobble Lady's food was caught in the act this morning, and the person paying him is even now being sought by the police. In retrospect——' he frowned '—I would probably have been wiser to have returned Lady to her trainer as soon as it became obvious Jennie would be safer here with me, but I wasn't thinking straight at the time! When I took Lady back yesterday afternoon I realised——' Maximillian frowned as Sophie gave a start of surprise. 'Where did you *think* I had gone yesterday afternoon?' he asked astutely.

With Celia Taylor! And instead he had been taking Gracious Lady back to her trainer.

'Ah.' Maximilian nodded understandingly as delicate colour darkened her cheeks. 'There was never anything between Celia and myself,' he assured her huskily. 'In fact,' he added self-derisively, 'I must be rather stupid——'

'You, Maximilian?' Sophie mocked with widely innocent eyes.

'—where Celia is concerned,' he finished drily, looking down at Sophie with raised brows. 'Because until that outburst from her a short time ago, I had no idea how she felt about me! I've certainly never thought of her in that way. Good God, she was Jo's little sister! And Jo and I were unsuited, God knows, but Celia and I would have been even more so!' He shook his head dismissively.

Leaving Sophie in no doubt whatsoever that no matter what Celia might have thought—or hoped!—to the contrary, there had never been any emotional or physical involvement between her and Maximilian.

'It seems I've been less than astute with all of my family since Jo died,' Maximilian continued with a grimace. 'I had no idea Jennie realised all about her mother and me—which was insulting to her intelligence. Jo and I only stayed together as long as we did because of Jennie. I don't know what went wrong between us exactly.' He shook his head sadly. 'Possibly we were too young when we married.' He shrugged. 'I was twenty and Jo was nineteen.'

Sophie knew all about marrying when you were too young!

'As we matured,' Maximilian sighed, 'we grew to want different things from life. With the money and success, Jo wanted a lifestyle to go with them—travel, a high-profile social life. And that wasn't me at all,' he shrugged. 'I tried to compromise, but Jo was having none of it, doing exactly what she wanted to do, when she wanted to. That's when the arguments began, until in the end there didn't even seem any point to them any longer. And once the rows stopped we went our separate ways, the only thing we apparently had left in common being Jennie. It wasn't easy, for any of us, I'm sure, living like that, but at the time it seemed better than the alternative,' he said sadly. 'And then Jo met someone else, someone she decided she wanted to marry.'

Sophie squeezed his arm comfortingly, could see how the failure of his marriage still affected him. Not because he had still loved his wife—she could see that he hadn't—but because it *had* been a failure.

'I was adamant,' he continued grimly, 'no matter what Jennie may have thought to the contrary, that Jo shouldn't have custody of Jennie. Jennie was in boarding school by this time, basically because I believed we could protect her from the situation between Jo and myself more easily that way, not because I ever wanted her to go away from me.' He gave a pained frown that Jennie should ever have thought that had been the reason. 'Jo was killed only six months after Jennie went away to school, the contention between us concerning Jennie's future still unsettled between us. So much so that I felt almost guilty for having got Jennie in that way,' he admitted gruffly, his eyes shadowed with the memory.

And that guilt, Sophie could see, had reflected on his future relationship with Jennie, making him hold back his love, when he should have drawn even closer because of Jo's death. Sophie really hoped Maximilian was right when he said that lack of understanding between himself and Jennie was over now; they both deserved so much more.

'When the threat was made on Jennie's life because of Lady I just went to pieces,' Maximilian admitted shakily now. 'The school holiday was looming, but I thought it best if she was kept away from me and Lady, that she would be harder to find if she stayed with Celia. I had forgotten at the time that I had asked your aunt to get you here for an interview,' he shook his head self-derisively. 'Although I'm glad I did now.' His gaze was warm on her flushed face. 'Otherwise you would just have received a telephone call telling you not to bother coming here at all, and then where would we all be?' he murmured huskily.

Where indeed? Sophie wasn't a hundred per cent certain where they were now; she still felt flustered by his proposal—certainly in no fit state to answer it yet!

'Jennie obviously had other ideas about going to Celia's,' she put in quickly.

Maximillian looked at her indulgently for her delaying tactics, seeming to guess at her near panic. 'Obviously,' he drawled, allowing her this small respite, 'Jennie had "other ideas" about a lot of things! It threw Paul's security completely when she just saddled Lady and rode her out of here!' He shook his head disgustedly.

So she had been right about Paul Wiseman's being the extra security here.

'Needless to say,' Maximilian added darkly, 'there has been a considerable shake-up there! And Paul is now on his way back to Lady's trainer to concentrate on security there. He's better with horses than people anyway!'

'I noticed that,' Sophie said ruefully, remembering how Paul had got her hackles up from the first with his not very subtle questioning.

Maximilian looked down at her teasingly. 'And I wondered if you might think he was a "good-looking young businessman"!' he drawled mockingly.

'Hardly,' she grimaced. 'I was too busy, as it happens, being captivated—in one way or another!—by a good-looking not-so-young businessman!' She gave him a mischievous look from beneath lowered lashes.

Maximilian burst out laughing. 'A "not-so-young businessman", hmm, "Jane"?' he repeated softly, his arms going about her.

'A *good-looking* not-so-young businessman, "Mr Rochester",' she corrected laughingly, sobering suddenly at the burning intensity of his gaze, realising that for the moment the laughter was over. 'Maximilian——'

'Sophie, I realise we haven't known each other very long,' he accepted huskily. 'But, as you said earlier, it's been an eventful few days. Emotionally charged,' he added grimly. 'But I knew that first night that there was something different about you——'

'Oh, there's something different about me, all right,' Sophie acknowledged self-derisively.

'Don't knock it, Sophie.' Maximilian's arms tightened about her waist. 'You're loyal, brutally frank, caring, honest——'

She frowned. 'A short time ago you believed I was totally *dishonest*,' she reminded him. 'That I had used my position here to give Brian that story.'

'It was because I guessed it was Burnett that I over-reacted to that,' he admitted with a sigh. 'I knew I loved you, and if you had been in this with Burnett then I knew you must be in love with him.' He grimaced. 'I kept you here in the first place, not just because of Jennie, but because my reaction to you was completely different than to any other woman I've ever met, and if, as it now appeared, you were in love with another man, then I was just left with the heartache of loving you.' He shook his head. 'I know it's no excuse for the things I said to you, but I was hurting very badly at that moment.'

Hurt before you were hurt—or *because* you were hurt; it was an instinctive response she couldn't possibly blame him for. 'But Jennie told you upstairs that it was you I loved,' she said ruefully.

'Among several other choice things,' he admitted with a grimace. 'She also told me you're doing your Open University course so that you can eventually go on to be a teacher?'

She had confided that to Jennie during the weekend. Teaching was something she had wanted to do before she met Malcolm, and she had found it was still something she wanted to do once that marriage was over. 'It's probably going to take me years,' she nodded. 'But I've done almost three years now——'

'I know that,' Maximilian told her gently. 'The report, remember?' he prompted at her puzzled look.

Did she remember! She also remembered how angry its very existence had made her feel.

'I know,' Maximilian soothed as he saw her expression. 'But Paul was only doing his job. But Sophie, there was nothing detrimental about you in that report. If anything it just made me admire you more.' He met her gaze with steady intensity. 'You have survived, Sophie, grown stronger, against overwhelming odds. There is no way I, or anyone else for that matter, could ever criticise you for that!' He put his hand beneath her chin, raising her face to his. 'If you'll marry me, Sophie, I'll do everything in my power to ensure that you can only grow stronger. You can go to university full-time, if you like, be a——'

'Maximilian, you don't have to offer me enticements.' She touched his cheek gently. 'I *want* to marry you. More than anything else,' she added huskily, knowing that she wouldn't accept his offer of going to university full-time, that she would carry on with her Open University course so that she could spend more time with her new husband. 'And I do mean *you*, Maximilian,' she continued intently. 'Your money——'

'Means nothing to you,' he finished assuredly. 'I know that, Sophie. I may have over-reacted about Burnett, but I have never doubted you in other ways. And although I'm sure Burnett is quite an innocuous chap, I've grown to dislike him intensely!' He frowned darkly.

'Um—about Brian...' Sophie began tentatively, playing with one of the buttons on the front of his shirt.

Maximilian immediately tensed. 'Yes?'

'Don't dislike him too intensely, because I have a feeling he may marry my cousin in time, and when he does the two of you are going to be related through marriage!' She grinned up at him.

'Your cousin——?' Maximillian looked dumbfounded. 'But—— '

'It's a long story, darling——'

'I remember you called me that last night,' he said gruffly. 'It made me feel quite hopeful for a while—which was probably another one of the reasons that damned newspaper upset me so much!'

'Forget about it.' She smoothed the frown from his brow. 'It isn't important. *We* are what's important.' She looked up at him with love-filled eyes. She wasn't leaving, never to see him again, after all, but was going to stay with him as his wife. She couldn't believe it! It was wonderful. Marvellous. Absolutely incredible!

'Yes,' he agreed gruffly as he saw the blaze of love in her eyes. 'And we have better things to do than worry about any of that. For one thing, you're wearing one of those pink shirts, and it seems a pity to waste it down here...' His eyebrows were raised questioningly. 'I'm sure, after our disturbed night, both of us could do with a little nap—eventually...'

Colour warmed her cheeks as his meaning was obvious. She could imagine nothing more wonderful than lying in his arms as they made love together, already knew how perfect they were going to be together. 'Are you sure you feel well enough?' She hesitated only out of concern for him. 'After all, you were very ill last night——'

'My darling Sophie——' he smiled down at her lovingly, holding her close against the hardness of his body, his desire evident '—I suspect I will feel like making love to you when I'm ninety and feeble!'

She returned his smile. 'In that case——' She broke off as the door opened without warning.

Jennie came bounding into the room. 'Well?' she demanded expectantly. 'Is Sophie going to be my stepmother or not?'

Maximilian groaned at the interruption, burying his face against Sophie's neck. 'Well, stepmother?' he murmured softly against Sophie's earlobe. 'Use your new authority to get rid of my daughter for a couple of hours—before I strangle her!'

Sophie chuckled softly, looking at Jennie over Maximilian's shoulder, tilting her head pointedly towards the door. Jennie nodded comprehendingly, their closeness being obvious, and quietly left the room again—after giving Sophie a thumbs-up sign!

Maximilian looked up dazedly at the quiet click of the door closing behind Jennie. 'Well, I'll be damned...' He looked down at Sophie admiringly. 'I knew you had hidden talents the night I met you—and I don't mean karate!' he added mockingly.

She grimaced at his reminder of the claim she had made that night. 'Talking of hidden talents...' she murmured pointedly.

He swung her effortlessly up into his arms. 'My room or yours?'

'Does it matter?' She put her arms lovingly about his neck, resting her cheek against his shoulder, quite content to go wherever he took her.

'No,' he acknowledged triumphantly. 'Nothing matters any more except the fact that we love each other. And I'm going to spend the rest of my life showing you just how much I love you,' he promised huskily.

Sophie didn't doubt it—or him—for a moment.

POSTCARDS FROM EUROPE™

HARLEQUIN PRESENTS™

Travel across Europe in 1994 with Harlequin Presents. Collect a new Postcards from Europe title each month!

Don't miss
YESTERDAY'S AFFAIR
by Sally Wentworth
Harlequin Presents #1668

Available in July wherever Harlequin Presents books are sold.

Hi!
I arrived safely in England and have found Nick. My <u>feelings for him</u> are as strong as ever, but he seems convinced that what we once shared belongs in the past. My heart won't accept that.
Love, Olivia

Fifty red-blooded, white-hot, true-blue hunks
from every State in the Union!

Look for MEN MADE IN AMERICA! Written by some of
our most popular authors, these stories feature fifty of
the strongest, sexiest men, each from a different state in
the union!

Two titles available every other month at your favorite
retail outlet.

In May, look for:

KISS YESTERDAY GOODBYE by Leigh Michaels (Iowa)
A TIME TO KEEP by Curtiss Ann Matlock (Kansas)

In June, look for:

ONE PALE, FAWN GLOVE by Linda Shaw (Kentucky)
BAYOU MIDNIGHT by Emilie Richards (Louisiana)

You won't be able to resist MEN MADE IN AMERICA!

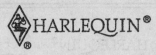

Harlequin Books requests the pleasure of your company this June in Eternity, Massachusetts, for WEDDINGS, INC.

For generations, couples have been coming to Eternity, Massachusetts, to exchange wedding vows. Legend has it that those married in Eternity's chapel are destined for a lifetime of happiness. And the residents are more than willing to give the legend a hand.

Beginning in June, you can experience the legend of Eternity. Watch for one title per month, across all of the Harlequin series.

HARLEQUIN BOOKS... NOT THE SAME OLD STORY!

HARLEQUIN®

PRESENTS Plus

Beth wants a child, but she doesn't want a husband.
Enter Alex Thiarchos. She seduces him and then
vanishes—it's a simple, yet rebellious, plan.
Except that life is *never* simple!

Samantha has worked for Guy Harwood for five years,
but it isn't until he reveals his desire to be a father
that she has the courage to make him a
daring proposition....

Fall in love with Alex and Guy—Beth and Samantha do!

Watch for

A Secret Rebellion by Anne Mather
Harlequin Presents Plus #1663

and

A Daring Proposition by Miranda Lee
Harlequin Presents Plus #1664

Harlequin Presents Plus
The best has just gotten better!

Available in July wherever Harlequin books are sold.

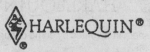

HARLEQUIN®

Don't miss these Harlequin favorites by some of our most
distinguished authors!
And now, you can receive a discount by ordering two or more titles!

HT #25551	THE OTHER WOMAN by Candace Schuler	$2.99	☐
HT #25539	FOOLS RUSH IN by Vicki Lewis Thompson	$2.99	☐
HP #11550	THE GOLDEN GREEK by Sally Wentworth	$2.89	☐
HP #11603	PAST ALL REASON by Kay Thorpe	$2.99	☐
HR #03228	MEANT FOR EACH OTHER by Rebecca Winters	$2.89	☐
HR #03268	THE BAD PENNY by Susan Fox	$2.99	☐
HS #70532	TOUCH THE DAWN by Karen Young	$3.39	☐
HS #70540	FOR THE LOVE OF IVY by Barbara Kaye	$3.39	☐
HI #22177	MINDGAME by Laura Pender	$2.79	☐
HI #22214	TO DIE FOR by M.J. Rodgers	$2.89	☐
HAR #16421	HAPPY NEW YEAR, DARLING		
	by Margaret St. George	$3.29	☐
HAR #16507	THE UNEXPECTED GROOM by Muriel Jensen	$3.50	☐
HH #28774	SPINDRIFT by Miranda Jarrett	$3.99	☐
HH #28782	SWEET SENSATIONS by Julie Tetel	$3.99	☐

Harlequin Promotional Titles

#83259	UNTAMED MAVERICK HEARTS	$4.99	☐
	(Short-story collection featuring Heather Graham Pozzessere, Patricia Potter, Joan Johnston)		

(limited quantities available on certain titles)

	AMOUNT	$
DEDUCT:	**10% DISCOUNT FOR 2+ BOOKS**	$
	POSTAGE & HANDLING	$
	($1.00 for one book, 50¢ for each additional)	
	APPLICABLE TAXES*	$ _____
	TOTAL PAYABLE	$ _____
	(check or money order—please do not send cash)	

To order, complete this form and send it, along with a check or money order for the
total above, payable to Harlequin Books, to: **In the U.S.:** 3010 Walden Avenue,
P.O. Box 9047, Buffalo, NY 14269-9047; **In Canada:** P.O. Box 613, Fort Erie, Ontario,
L2A 5X3.

Name: _____

Address: _____ City: _____

State/Prov.: _____ Zip/Postal Code: _____

*New York residents remit applicable sales taxes.
 Canadian residents remit applicable GST and provincial taxes.